THE SILVER CAGE

the SILVER CAGE

ANONYMOUS

Text copyright © 2017
All rights reserved

This is a work of fiction. All of the characters, organizations, and events portrayed in this novel are either products of the author's imagination or are used in a fictitious manner. Any resemblance to actual persons, living or dead, or actual events is purely coincidental.

There is no trap so deadly as the trap you set for yourself.

—RAYMOND CHANDLER, *THE LONG GOODBYE*

1

CALEB

Last night, I dreamed that I died. Or maybe I dreamed it this morning. The lucid scene felt close to my waking, the sensations still clinging to me as I stared at the ceiling.

In the dream, I was at church with my mother. My father and sister were absent. It was the church I had attended in my youth and everything was just as I remember it. We were seated at our usual pew, waiting for the service to start, when an unfamiliar man entered. I could paint his face, it's so vivid in my mind: Tightly curling brown hair, watery blue eyes, and reddish-brown stains on his cheekbones and forehead.

We exchanged a long, intense stare.

The man passed in front of my mother and sat beside her. He draped his arm across her lap and gripped her knee. She stiffened and looked at me.

"Caleb," she whispered fearfully.

I pushed the man's hand off my mother's lap and leaned toward him. "Find another place to sit," I said, my voice low with menace.

The man rose and moved to the pew behind us. It made me uneasy, being unable to see him, and I sensed that some violence was coming.

I heard a metallic *clack*, like the sound of a revolver's hammer dropping, and my mother slumped beside me. With a cold, visceral shock, I realized that she had been shot.

I hope I'm not next, I thought, and the cold feeling spread outward from the nape of my neck. Then I understood that I had already been shot. I reached back and my fingertips touched ruined, wet flesh, blasted open. *This is it*, I told myself. I felt a momentary panic, and then I was glad.

There was no pain, as if all my nerves had been blown out of the crater in my neck. My vision dimmed and I seemed to be drifting downward softly, peacefully, my consciousness draining fast. I was accepting and relieved.

I woke with a broad numb patch at the back of my neck.

I lay in bed for a long time, processing the experience, and then I listened to the message on my phone. It was from my agent.

"Cal," she said, "hi. Just a small thing. The journalist coming today isn't the one I told you to expect. She had a death in the family. So expect someone else. I couldn't get a name for you, but the editor said she would be calling her best writer, okay? They're really excited. Let me know how it goes."

I sat up in bed and cleared my throat before returning the call.

"Cal?" My agent sounded apprehensive. She knew what was coming.

"Hi, Beth. Look, I'm not feeling the interview, what with the change."

"Cal, talk to me. What's the problem?"

I hated when Beth tried to handle me. Worse, I hated when she handled me. A month earlier, she had convinced me to agree to the profile in the face of my direct refusal. And I had only agreed after researching the journalist who would be writing the profile, after reading her stuff and determining that she was too glib to even scratch the surface of my situation.

That journalist would have phoned in a feeble version of the profile that half a dozen others had written: Author Caleb Bright retires after writing three contemporary classics, moves to the mountains of Colorado, takes up painting; friends and family comment on his artistic nature and deep religiosity; everyone cites stress as his reason for ending his literary career.

But I wouldn't be dealing with that journalist anymore, and I don't like unknowns.

"Cancel it," I said, "or maybe we can postpone until—"

"She's taking two months off. You know the piece is for December."

"You're springing this on me. Why am I only hearing about this now?" I threw back the sheets and began to pace. After nine years working with Beth, I had learned to recognize her tactics, though I never got better at evading them.

"Of course not. They only told me yesterday. Really, Cal, it doesn't matter. *The New Yorker* is big for us. This is exciting. And the fact that they're looking to include you in their '2016 in Letters' issue . . ." She trailed off.

"You can say it." I stopped in front of the window. The morning was peerless: Sunlight breaking through mist, enflaming the yellow aspen leaves. I rarely woke early enough to catch the sunrise. The dream had woken me. I rubbed the back of my neck. "Say it," I repeated. "It means I'm somehow still relevant."

"I'm just thrilled that the re-release did so well. People loved your forward."

"Is the new journalist a woman? Do you know?"

"You are such a playboy." Beth laughed. She knew that she had won. She knew that she could play the relevancy card to scare me into anything. Sometimes, I even thought she knew that I had never really wanted to stop publishing—that I was desperately afraid of being forgotten. My robust literary career hung on the success of three novels. Would I still be on the shelves in ten years? In thirty? "I honestly don't know," she continued, "but I told them you prefer women."

"Good." I was sure the editor had gotten a kick out of that, but I didn't care.

"We'll talk after you two meet," Beth said.

"I'll e-mail."

"Great. Keep me posted."

We hung up and I gazed dejectedly out the window. The memory of the dream kept pulsing against me, a strange resonance, and I felt sick to my stomach.

I skipped my morning run, showered, and made the bed. I was barely able to go through the motions. Maybe the dream played a small part in my mood, but unhappiness was a mainstay for me. I thought about my books. I thought about the state of my life and I bucked against it. *I'll publish*, I told myself. *I'll do it—to hell with the consequences.* Then I shuddered and fury rose up my throat like bile.

I dressed in dark jeans and a black sweater to suit my mood. Some mornings, when I got my coffee and dove into writing, I almost felt good. The act of writing produced a forgetfulness that carried me along, out of my life, into a current of imagination. That day, though, I had to wait for the journalist, I had to think about my dream, and Beth's call and comments trapped me in misery. I couldn't help but consider my career, and a terrible sense of futility surged through me, rage scraping at its edges.

I took my coffee to the deck, and my Bible. I let the well-worn book fall open to a Psalm. My eyes wandered the page, seeking comfort. I always found something—a little something to hold on to—if only the fact that after this life came a life without pain, fear, hatred, or guilt.

I pictured Heaven as a field where I would wake one day, warm in the tall grass, and see a man seated at a distance. He would have his back to me and he would be looking out at the landscape. I would come awake slowly, into perfect happiness, and, when I was ready, I would stand up and go to him.

I would spend the rest of forever in that summer country.

The sun crawled higher into the sky until it pierced my eyes. I took my reading inside then, and I heard tires on the drive at noon.

2

MICHAEL

I tossed the mammoth book onto my desk. It was so ridiculously fat and heavy, even in paperback, that momentum carried it right off the edge. It sailed into Furio's doggy bed and clipped the edge of his skull. He woke with a yelp and skittered onto the hardwood floor, sliding and scrabbling comically.

I am convinced that corgis can't look serious doing anything.

"That's good," I mumbled around the toothbrush protruding from my mouth. I crouched and smoothed a hand over Furio's head. "Are you okay? Sorry about that. Blame Caleb Bright and his encyclopedic novels."

I rinsed my mouth in the bathroom and hurried back to the desk. I leaned over my laptop and typed out the line—*I am convinced that corgis can't look serious doing anything*—and considered the blog post I would build around it. I could make it cute-funny. I could include pictures of Furio's antics. I could even take it toward the serious-sentimental, touching on the real companionship dogs offer.

"Everyone can relate to that. Dogs. Pets. Non-judgmental companions. And they *need* us." I was typing furiously, adding snippets to the document and mumbling to myself as I did. "They need us for basic survival. Food, water. Hell, we take them out to poop. We take care of them. It's a bonding thing. Pets are like infants that never grow up. Forever children. We love them for that."

I paused and grinned. Barely a week ago, Furio had found and consumed some sort of vine-like weed in the backyard. The eating of it apparently hadn't been a problem, but when it came time for the plant to pass, he couldn't get it out. He had crouched pitifully, a fragment of poop hanging from his behind, shuffled forward and crouched again, and rubbed his butt along the grass, all to no avail.

I had finally noticed his predicament when I heard him whimpering. I had tried coaching him through it, kneeling at his side and patting his rump. "You gotta push," I had told him. "It's just poop. You can do it." But he couldn't do it, and his big black eyes were damp and he was frightened.

So, it had quickly become evident that I needed to assist my dog by manually extracting the plant from his butt. And I had done it, and he had been so grateful afterward, licking my face and tearing around the yard.

Something passed between us, I typed, *something that can only pass between a man and his dog. We had endured the vine-poop together, and we weren't ashamed. We were stronger, braver—*

"Weren't you supposed to leave at nine?" Nicole appeared in the doorway. She was holding a hanger with an ironed dress shirt and frowning. "Why was Furio crying?"

"Caleb Bright almost took him out." I fetched the novel from the floor and plopped it on the desk. "I'm ready. I'm going." I closed my laptop and tucked it under my arm, and I patted my keys and wallet.

"Did you finish that?" She eyed the book. "Is that what you're wearing?" She eyed my shirt. It was a graphic tee with a pixelated sword above the caption I DON'T WORK OUT, I LEVEL UP.

My girlfriend was ever ready to remind me that I dressed like a sixteen year old and that Authentic Vans and gamer T-shirts "look sad and desperate on a twenty-five-year-old man." I narrowed my eyes. There was a blog post in that, for sure . . . something about the way we conform to social standards as we age, about branding, systemization, corporate control of our—

"Mike?"

I blinked. "I'm comfortable. And what if he games? This shirt could strike up a ton of conversation." I wrinkled my nose. "Besides, Oxford shirts make me sweat for some reason."

"Could it be that they make you think of responsibility?" Nicole gave a longsuffering sigh. "So you didn't finish the book?"

"Nearly. I skimmed the end. I'll finish it tonight. And I did read the other two. We're not going to talk about his books, anyway. This is an icebreaker day, get to know each other, schedule stuff. And I have a bunch of questions on here." I tapped my MacBook. "I'll be guiding the conversation."

"Okay. Well, I put gas in the Jeep. Call me if you get lost."

"I won't get lost." I displayed my iPhone.

"Red Feather Lakes is the actual boonies. Some roads might not be mapped."

"Uncharted territory." I kissed her cheek on my way past. "Adventure."

Furio swirled around our feet, sensing my departure. I gave him a kiss, too.

Most days, Nicole was more like a mother than a girlfriend to me, but I couldn't hold that against her. She kept me on track in so many ways. Over the past three years, she had helped redirect my explosive energy into lucrative outlets—streaming, blogging—and, under her more mature influence, I had made the leap from ramen-eating apartment-owner to sometimes-square-meal-eating co-homeowner.

Between my blog, stream, freelance journalism, and Nicole's steady work for a pharmaceutical company, we did well. Very well. But it hadn't always been that way. On one of our early dates, I had taken her to Q'doba and my card had been declined. Our food had already been prepared; it was supposed to be my treat. As I fumbled through my empty wallet, the cashier had taken stock of my situation. "Don't worry about it," he had finally said. Still, it had taken me a while to grasp that he was giving us free food.

In those days, my skill set had included playing computer games, having funny-stupid thoughts that I never wrote down, and being the fastest balloon tier at the party warehouse where I worked, and Nicole had stuck with me.

I guess that's what couples mean when they talk about history. History is the shit that keeps meaning something when everything else starts to mean nothing.

The drive from Boulder to Red Feather Lakes took two hours, which gave me time to build up a solid case of nerves. It was one thing, being social and witty online with thousands of strangers watching me play games, and quite another thing to meet a high-profile author and to behave like a smart, educated adult.

And I was smart, and I was educated. I had graduated with highest honors and double majors in English and Journalism. After starting my blog—a slice-of-life, humor blog—I had branched into freelance feature writing, and my voice and degree had landed my work in a cluster of small magazines and papers. I'd built from there, and after a year I had managed to get a personal essay into *The Atlantic*, a similar piece in *New York Magazine*, and a commentary on the culture of PC gaming in *The New Yorker*.

Which brings us to Caleb Bright and the call I got five days ago.

My cell had rung at about four in the afternoon and, at the time, I was streaming a competitive Overwatch match. I had seven thousand viewers, which is high for my channel, and I was on a winning streak. Walking away from the match had meant losing a hard-won rank and pulling the plug on a majorly successful broadcast, but one doesn't simply ignore an editor at *The New Yorker*.

"Shit," I had said. "I hate to do this, bros, but I absolutely have to take this."

The chat in my channel spammed sad faces.

I frowned, shut off my broadcasting software, and took the call.

The editor, Eliza Harel, had hastily explained that they (*The New Yorker*) needed a journalist (me) ASAP (in five days) for an important profile (Caleb Bright). The journalist who was supposed to write the profile had taken two months off for a family emergency, and the magazine didn't want to shuffle dates or arrangements because the author was already "jumpy."

"Jumpy how?" I had asked.

"He's been out of the publishing scene for a few years. He's leery of media. You'll have to research all that. The thing is, you're in his neck of the woods and we loved your writing in that video game article. We're looking for—"

"It was PC games, not console—"

"Right. We loved it. We want *that* voice—young, inquisitive. All the profiles on this guy have been pretty stale. I mean, what is he doing now? Is he writing? What really made him stop? We think you can bring the outsider perspective."

The outsider perspective. She had meant that I, a full-time streamer and computer game enthusiast, couldn't possibly moonlight as a literary type. I was the second choice, the last-minute backup. But I was okay with that. *The New Yorker* had called *me*, soliciting a story. I was literary enough to know how huge that was.

We had talked specifics for about ten minutes and exchanged contact info, and then I'd had five days to read

Bright's three giant novels, a smattering of criticism, and a few of the stale profiles Eliza had mentioned.

I had also examined the most recent picture I could find online, which showed the author at a signing in 2010. He was tall and black-haired, with golden-tan skin and an unsmiling face. His eyes were dark and serious. Though he was in the process of shaking hands with a reader, he was glaring at whoever had snapped the photo.

"Jumpy." I spoke into the silence of my Jeep. "He's just jumpy, and people who feel anxious act mean, like cornered animals." But I would show him that I meant no harm. I would approach slowly, hands up, and he would learn to trust me. He would tell me what made him laugh, what troubled him, why he had come to Colorado when all of his family lived on the East Coast, and why he had walked away from a tremendous literary career and disappeared into the blue.

Then I would write a profile so fine that major magazines would be begging me for articles for years to come.

(That quote about the best-laid plans is appropriate here.)

Despite Nicole's fears, Google Maps had imaged all the roads leading to Caleb Bright's house. I drove north, then west into the mountains, and I rolled down my window to let in the autumn air. It smelled like campfire. It was late September, the time when the aspens turn, and I would have been freezing without my jacket.

I toyed with first lines as I pulled up the long gravel drive.

In September, the road to Red Feather is paved with golden leaves . . .

Too saccharine.

Caleb Bright lives off the beaten path . . .

Cliché.

I am sweating as I pull up to . . .

No. Just no on beginning with bodily odors.

The first thing you see when you reach Caleb Bright's property is the lake.

It was broad and clear and that day it reflected the glacier blue of the sky, a shade almost aquamarine, and the yolk yellow leaves of hundreds of aspen, which shrouded the hill and partially hid the house.

The log cabin style home melded into the countryside. I saw no other houses or docks around the lake, or anywhere in my field of vision, meaning the author must have owned everything I could see. The thought unnerved me. This was his domain and I felt small in that expansive landscape.

As I climbed out of the car and headed up the walk, I got the distinct sense that I was being watched. A motion at the window caught my attention. I glanced over and down I went, the ground rushing up, a starburst of pain exploding in front of my eyes.

3

CALEB

I PADDED THROUGH THE FRONT room and flicked back the curtain, and I went cold in the face. I must have turned a sickening shade of ash.

The journalist wasn't a woman or even much of a man. Maybe he wasn't the journalist at all. He had the look of one of the unkempt young writers that sometimes found their way to my house, as if it were Mecca, as if their pilgrimage would end with anything but a door slamming in their faces.

But it wasn't his youthful, untidy appearance that struck me.

No, he was a ghost from the past. Here, alone, in this remote place, and without any happiness, I was finally losing my mind.

Good, I immediately thought, and the dream tickled at the back of my neck. Madness, like death, is a sort of freedom—the mind breaking loose and running.

A shout startled me.

The man fell face-first on my walkway, throwing up an arm at the last second. A laptop tumbled from his grip, clattering on the flagstones, and he curled into a ball and clutched his head. I stared, stunned for a moment. Then I yanked open the door.

"What are you doing here?" I snapped. My heart pummeled against my chest and my hands shook.

He uncurled slowly, planted his hands on the path, and peered up at me. Whatever he saw made his mouth fall open.

"Who are you?" I demanded, grating out the words.

His eyes were red, watering with pain and embarrassment, and blood oozed from a cut on his cheekbone.

"I'm sorry," he said. I pressed against the door, away from him. He crawled to his laptop and lifted it. With a wavering hand, he touched the gash on his cheek. "Shit." He winced and rose unsteadily. He looked at his bloodstained fingers, at me. I could see his idea of an introductory handshake evaporating, leaving an awkward blank in its wake.

"What do you want?" I said.

"I'm—my name is Michael Beck. I'm here for *The New Yorker*." His hand twitched with the effort it took not to extend it.

I recoiled into the house. "Are you? How do I know that?"

The flush in his face deepened. "Oh, I—let me get my ID, my—"

"Forget it. Come in." I was losing control of the situation, of myself. He had fallen. He was bleeding. "Stay here." I moved briskly to the bathroom and returned with Neosporin and bandages. I dropped them on the coffee table between us. "Use those. Sit."

I pointed to the couch and then I went out, retrieving my cigarettes on the way. I slammed the deck door behind me. I could only hope the gesture communicated my wishes: Leave me alone out here.

The cold wrapped around me and the rough boards of the deck pricked at my soles. I smoked and stared at my phone, debating a call to Beth. The journalist was a problem. I should send him away—and I would, as soon as I reasonably could—

but he had fallen and split his face open on my walk, which changed things. And then he had apologized. My God, he had apologized for smashing *his* face into *my* landscaping. Who did that? My stomach pitched.

I glanced into the house. He was seated on the couch, hunched forward.

I burned through another cigarette and went in. The tang of tobacco clung to my tongue and clothes. "You startled me," I said, striding toward the window. I didn't look at him. I looked out at the walkway. "Is something wrong with the path?"

"No. No, I just lost my balance."

"I'll look at it tomorrow." I reopened the front door and pretended to study the path. "Yeah. Tomorrow."

He was quiet, and so I finally had to turn and look at him. He had created the most ridiculous covering for his wound—a square of cotton folded under two Band-Aids, the bandages forming a bulky X. He had his computer open on his lap. The screen was black. His shoulders slumped.

"Well?" I said.

He cleared his throat. "Yes. Sorry. We can get started."

"Fire away." I sat in the armchair opposite the couch and wondered how obvious it was that I wanted to be nowhere near him. Could he see me pressing into the chair to achieve max distance, and tactically keeping the coffee table between us?

"Well, it's nice to meet you, Mr. Bright."

"Cal." I blurted out my preferred name before I realized I didn't want him calling me anything too familiar.

"Okay. Cal. Let me just . . ." He fiddled with his unresponsive MacBook while I white-knuckled the chair and stared at him, letting the impression sink into me. He had silky, fawn-brown hair, streaked gold by the sun or by luck, and thick like oil paint. His eyes were liquid, the color of his hair. He was pale, on the thin side, but his shoulders were broad and veins roped over his hands.

And then there was the set of his jaw, so familiar, stubbornness barely cloaking uncertainty. The fall had rattled him badly. I could see that now.

"Are you okay?" I made my voice indifferent.

"Yes, thank you. I had everything on here." He ran his fingers over the laptop. "I think it's damaged."

"I'm sorry." I grimaced. "What a pain. Are you sure?"

"Well, hopefully the hard drive is okay. It's just not booting up." He depressed the power button again. The apple on the case remained unlit.

"Do you need to go to a walk-in? How hard did you . . ." I gestured toward the door. I had seen how hard he had hit his face, and I supposed it was possible that he had fractured a facial bone. Maybe he would bring a lawsuit after I cancelled the profile. That would be just my luck.

"Uh, I don't think so. It's throbbing, but it's sort of numb, too." He prodded the bandaging and flinched.

"Don't touch it," I hissed.

His hand flew to his lap.

Throbbing, but sort of numb. He had a way with words. I wanted to roll my eyes. Wasn't the magazine supposed to be deploying its *best* writer? I should have known that was only a line. The man before me had arrived with nothing but a laptop, now broken, and he was dressed like a college student. I couldn't decipher his T-shirt, unless it was intended as overstated irony. He very clearly did not work out and the shade of his skin suggested he lived by the light of a computer screen.

He caught me studying the shirt. "Do you game?" He smiled hopefully.

"No. Never." My lips curled. "When did you fly in? The altitude might be affecting you. Are you feeling lightheaded?"

"Oh, I live in Boulder. I drove up. I'm fine."

I raised an eyebrow. "Are you a freelancer?"

"Yeah."

"How exactly did you come by this assignment?"

"Um, an editor called me." I could tell he was leaving out part of the story. "The other writer had—"

"I know."

"I've written for them. *The New Yorker.* They like my stuff."

"Do you write for them regularly?"

"Not . . . regularly. A little. Once, so far." He looked at his feet. "This will be my second piece for them. And I live in the area, so."

"How convenient." I stood and put more distance between us. I went to the front windows, spread open the curtains, and examined the walk again. All the flagstones appeared even, as far as I could see. Anyway, this pitiful creature would never bring a lawsuit. He wasn't the type. He had no teeth, no spine. He wasn't a New Yorker or even a New Englander. Meanwhile, I had been raised in an upscale corner of Massachusetts where people didn't smile at one another and the high school students all but turned into Tonya Harding in the battle for valedictorian.

I had taken that title, by the way.

"I'm excited for—"

"I think we had better aim to start another day," I interrupted. "Next weekend, if that works. You should get your face looked at, and your computer."

"Oh, I—"

"I'm sure you want to get that handled as soon as possible."

"I guess I could drop it off at the Apple Store on my way home." He kept trying to slide into an informal tone, as if we would suddenly be heading to a sports bar together. I felt sorry for him, momentarily. "Have you eaten?"

"Yes," I lied.

"Okay. Maybe we could talk about scheduling before I go." He patted his pockets for a pen and paper he did not possess.

"Let's play it by ear."

"Sure, we can do that." He stood and laughed feebly. "Ah, I'm sorry. This really didn't go as planned."

"No need to apologize. I'll have to look at this tomorrow." I opened the door and went out, walking down the path and watching my feet as I did. He had no choice but to follow me. I was kicking him out in the kindest way possible.

"Next weekend, then? I can come earlier. Whatever works for you." He tried to walk beside me. I veered onto the grass.

"Next weekend is fine."

"Should we exchange numbers?"

"Oh, my agent handles all that." I smiled tersely. "Have your editor friend talk to her. We'll get it sorted out."

At last, I saw the awareness dawning on him—I was giving him the boot, permanently—but instead of appearing angry, he looked crestfallen and confused, like a kicked dog. "Sure, okay. Look, I'm sorry again—"

"Please." I raised my hands for silence and went back inside, alone.

4

CALEB

I STARTED DRINKING AFTER MICHAEL Beck left—two fingers of whiskey—and continued steadily through the afternoon, never quite drunk, but far from sober by evening.

One of the many dangers of drinking alone is that you have no one else by whom to gauge your level of intoxication.

Around seven, I called my ex-wife. The setting sun was melting over the deck, into my whiskey glass, and it was the most exquisite shade of fire. I swirled it into the alcohol and lit a cigarette. I had gone through a pack in half a day.

"Caleb?" Coral answered. Coral enjoyed reminding me of my Biblical namesake, though she knew full well that I preferred to be called Cal.

"I want to talk to Caleb Junior." Caleb Jr. was our five-year-old son. In the south, families have a literal obsession with naming sons Daddy Junior. I had done everything in my power to spare my son from that fate, but his mother, grandmother, and aunts had banded together against me, and I had lost. Still, I made my stand by refusing to call him Junior, which everyone else did. What a degrading nickname, if you think about it.

I must have slurred my request, because Coral snapped, "Are you drunk?"

It was difficult to speak, not because of the drinks. I moved the receiver away from my mouth and breathed deeply, slowly.

"Are you there? I'm going to hang up."

"Let me talk to him," I said.

"Do you know what time it is?"

To be fair, I had lost track of the time, but it didn't really matter. Morning, noon, or night, Coral found excuses to keep me from speaking to my son.

I saw him less than once a year, and then only for two or three weeks when I was visiting my parents. We would all get together at their summer home in Martha's Vineyard—me, my ex-wife, Caleb Jr., my father, mother, and sister—and in that supervised, highly Christian setting, I would be allowed to spend time with my boy.

"He's my son," I mumbled.

"Okay, you've obviously been drinking. Junior is in bed. I'm hanging up now."

"Coral, can we—"

She ended the call.

I slid my glass and phone onto the table and leaned over my knees. I hadn't spoken her name, imploringly or otherwise, in quite a long time, and for a moment I thought I might vomit.

But God, I missed my son's little voice, the immature Rs that made him sound like a tiny English gentleman, and his outsized vocabulary.

Inside, I emptied my glass in the sink.

I had made myself pathetic in front of her, which meant I'd had enough to drink.

I built a fire, carried my laptop to the couch, and, at last, did the thing I had been resisting all day: I Googled Michael Beck.

I found his blog, called MikeCheck, which contained his picture and biography in the sidebar. *Mike Beck is a full-time streamer (twitch.tv/mikecheck), PC game enthusiast, corgi owner, and freelance journalist who lives with his girlfriend in Boulder, CO.*

There was a picture of his dog and, presumably, his girlfriend.

There was also a feed showing his latest tweet, written two hours earlier. I barked out a laugh when I read it. **Have you ever had someone look at you like you're an actual turd? I know that feel today.**

The blog posts dated back to 2014. I chuckled helplessly over the titles: *When You're Low-Key Worried About Male-Pattern Hair Loss; Dicks Out For Harambe (A Meme Explained); A Guide to Living On Children's Breakfast Cereals; Why Does Air Travel Make Everyone Greasy?; Why Does Fast Food Return to a Non-Nutritive State if Saved For 2+ Hours?; "Just the Feet" – One Man's Journey With Pot Edibles.*

I expected the posts themselves to be borderline ridiculous, but they weren't. He approached each topic with the same painfully earnest attitude I had seen earlier that day. The humorous touches were light, natural, and in places the writing hit thoughtful, somber notes. He had hundreds of comments per post.

As I was reading, a new tweet appeared in the feed. **Live in five – twitch.tv/mikecheck – gaming on some DayZ.**

I clicked the link. It took me to a page with an embedded media player and a chat box on the side. And there he was, in the corner of the screen, seated at a desk and still sporting his silly bandage. He also wore a headset with a microphone.

"What up, my dudes?" he said. He sounded miserable. I dialed up the volume and glanced at the chat. Someone typed: **What happened to your face?** Dozens of others echoed the question. Some laughed; some posted sad faces and hearts.

What had I stumbled on to?

As I watched, the number of viewers ticked up to one thousand, then two thousand, and soon—if the counter wasn't lying—five thousand. The chat scrolled so rapidly I could barely read it.

He's live!
LUL your face
Bro what happened?
Sad Mike looks sad
DayZ today? Zzz
Incoming running simulator
FeelsBadMan

"Mods, can we go sub mode for a while?" he said. "Sorry, guys. I can't deal with a fast chat tonight."

A line of text appeared—*now in subscriber-only mode*—and the chat slowed.

"Thanks. Uh, my face . . ." He logged in to a game, which filled the bulk of the media player. "I fell on it. I fell like you only fall when you're four. You know when you're a kid and you try to walk but you basically just tip over?" He demonstrated, dropping his arm in a plank-like motion. I grinned faintly and shook my head. He had, indeed, fallen just like that.

The chat spammed laughter and sympathy.

"Laugh it up." He smirked. "You're all due for a fall one of these days. Everyone falls; it's just a matter of when. Of course, I fell right in front of someone. Super hard."

I found it much easier to watch him when he wasn't seated in my home, sucking all the oxygen out of the room. And, watching him like that, I was able to appreciate the little ways in which he differed from Jamie. Michael was older, of course, and funnier. Jamie had been so serious. I could tell that Michael loved to laugh and seemed to enjoy socializing, if only from the safety of what appeared to be his basement. Jamie had always shied away from people. Except for me.

I gripped my head.

All the ghosts were coming out to play tonight.

I felt suddenly enervated, as if the toll of the day were finally hitting me: The death dream, Michael Beck, my abortive call to Coral. Why had I called her, anyway? I knew that she would never come around. Maybe I had needed to be sure, though, beyond any doubt, that my chances at normal happiness were gone.

And they were—they were gone.

"Shitty days, dudes. We all have them." Michael was talking to the people typing in chat, but he could have been talking to me. "And yes, we're playing DayZ tonight. This is a bonus stream cause I didn't expect to be home, and I want to zone out."

A fragment of music played and the words *New Subscriber: Eternal Kek* scrolled along the top of the window. I tilted my head.

"Hey, thanks for the subscription, Eternal Kek." Michael forced a smile. "Welcome to the team. I really appreciate the support. Guys, can we get some hot mics in the chat for a brand new subscriber? Thanks again, man. I hope you enjoy the content."

The chat filled with tiny icons, which appeared to be flaming microphones with the letter M on them. I barely understood what I was seeing.

Next came a ringtone-like sound with the words *Invocation: $3.00 Feel better Mikey you're right everyone falls chin up dude.*

"Thanks for the three dollars, Invocation. Exactly, man. Everyone falls. Everyone poops. Thankfully I didn't fall *and* poop. Silver linings."

He continued to play the game, which appeared to involve running through a vast wilderness while collecting guns and avoiding zombies, and strangers from the Internet continued to subscribe and donate various sums of money.

I scrolled down the page.

I noticed the subscription button ($4.99), the same photo from his blog, some text detailing his computer specs and broadcast schedule (five days a week, seven hours a day), and a donation graphic in the form of a hand-drawn tip jar. *Click the jar to donate. Donations are appreciated but never required.*

I clicked on the image, which rerouted me to PayPal. In the donation box, I typed 2000.00 and the message: *Buy yourself a new laptop.* I left the name area blank.

I confirmed the payment and returned to the stream.

Some moments passed before the ringtone sounded and the notification appeared at the top of the window. The viewers noticed it before Michael, who was fighting zombies. The chat exploded.

2k!?!?!?!
OMG MIKE $2000 DONATION
MIKE R U BLIND
WTF

I chuckled and steepled my fingers under my chin. You might have thought I had given the chat two thousand dollars; they were so excited. They began to spam an icon of Michael's face wearing a blindfold.

"Dudes, I know I got a dono," he said, exasperated. "Gimme five seconds. It's hard to look at two monitors when you have zombies coming at you like—" He waved his arms wildly and I laughed harder. Then he saw the donation.

His smile fell and his eyes went round.

"Oh, holy shit."

On the screen, zombies mauled his character to death. He wasn't watching.

"Ho-ly *shit*," he repeated. I wondered how much of his shock was genuine and how much was an act for the viewers. Since the largest donation I had seen that evening was thirty dollars, I assumed he was sincerely stunned. And I liked it. From the seclusion of my mountain home, I had rendered him speechless.

He scrubbed his face and covered his mouth. His eyes flickered between monitors.

"Wow. Anonymous, not even dropping a name. Dude. Thank you. I don't know what to say. Lemme read this message." His expression changed again, subtly—a little hitch from awe to embarrassment, which I doubted anyone else noticed. "Okay, um, anonymous with the 2K donation says . . . buy yourself a new laptop." He coughed. "Dang, dude. That is super generous. I seriously don't know what to say."

His eyes avoided the webcam.

"Oh. Zombies gang-banged me." He refocused on the game. "I feel like I can't even play right now."

But he tried, valiantly, and I watched until I couldn't stand it anymore.

Then I called my agent and left a voicemail.

"Beth," I said. "I never, ever want to see that journalist again."

5

MICHAEL

The call came on Monday morning and it went more or less as I had expected. Eliza Harel from *The New Yorker* apologized profusely and lied for Caleb Bright's agent, who had probably lied for him. "There was some kind of misunderstanding," the editor said. "Apparently, the author wanted to cancel the profile before we even sent you out there. I am so, so sorry for the inconvenience."

"So there isn't going to be a profile?" I said.

"Well, we're working on it. But Michael, we *love* your voice. We'll be in touch, okay?" She hurried me off the phone. Every editor I have ever communicated with possessed that ability: The ability to end a call at guillotine speed.

I was already awake—with a dog and a girlfriend who left for work at seven, I rarely slept in—and seated at my desk. Since my laptop was out of commission, I opened Notepad on one of my gaming desktops. I cracked my knuckles and smashed out a line: *Caleb Bright is a son of a bitch.*

There. That was all the profile he needed.

I would never forget the way he had looked at me, with a mixture of horror and revulsion, as if I were a mutant. He had cringed away from me, practically pressing against the farthest wall or piece of furniture when we were in the same room. What had I done wrong? Maybe I should have taken Nicole's advice and dressed more formally, but even so, a T-shirt and jeans didn't merit the author's behavior.

He had come off as slightly psychotic. Did he have a blood phobia? Had I committed the ultimate *faux pas* by smashing my face into his walkway?

By turns, he had seemed angry with me and scared of me.

And then there was his appearance, so greatly changed from the 2010 photo. He had the same black hair, but it was long now, unkempt, sweeping into his eyes and hanging in thick shocks around his neck. His skin was pallid, the kiss of sun gone, and his face was gaunt and filled with shadows.

My feelings swerved toward pity.

Was he sick? He had looked sick, like he was dying of some consumptive illness.

I had terrorized him unintentionally, I was sure of it—but how?

The final, most infuriating piece of the puzzle had come later, during my stream: Two thousand dollars from the only person who knew about my broken laptop, i.e. Caleb Bright. I hadn't even told Nicole about the laptop. She had grilled me so mercilessly about the meeting (and my injury) that I'd had no desire to rehash anything extra.

I also hadn't dropped off the laptop at the Apple Store because I felt sure I could fix it myself, or at least recover the hard drive.

So the two thousand dollars could only have come from him. But he had fired me. He had planned to fire me the moment he'd escorted me out of his house, if not sooner. And he didn't seem the type to drop two thousand dollars out of guilt. No, he didn't seem the type at all. I remembered his black, furious stare, and I shuddered. When I had first laid eyes on him, I had truly thought he might attack me.

I swiveled slowly in my office chair, one way, then the other.

I tapped out a tweet on my phone. **No stream today – personal day**.

I refreshed Furio's water and food, made sure his doggy door was open, wrote a check for two thousand dollars, and drove back to Red Feather.

6

MICHAEL

By the time I knocked on Caleb Bright's door, I had worked myself into a towering rage. I needed the anger, like armor. And maybe I should have invested in real body armor. He might be a gun-owner. He might shoot me. Out here, in the middle of nowhere, there would be no witnesses. He could claim self-defense.

The door swung open and I fell back a step.

This time, he looked more alarmed than angry.

"What do you want?" he said, shaking his head.

I thrust the check at him. He accepted it reluctantly, read it, and frowned.

"Why did you give me that?"

"Never mind." He crumpled the check. "You tripped on my walkway and broke your computer. It was the least I could do."

"You fired me. I want to know why."

He sneered and turned his back on me, and for a moment I thought he was going to shut the door. He folded his arms, lowered his head. When he turned to face me again, he was wearing a polite and uncomfortable smile. "No, I didn't."

"You cancelled the profile." I jammed my hands into my pockets. It had been chilly in Boulder and it was bitter in the mountains. Worse, my anger was giving way to embarrassment. I felt stupid for coming. Soon, my voice would start to shake, the way it always does when I try to confront someone. "Look, it's fine. I just want to know why, you know? For my future work. If I did something wrong . . ."

"I didn't cancel it. There must have been some misunderstanding." He shrugged and gazed past me, into the trees. His faint smile turned apologetic. "I told my agent I didn't want anyone *else* writing the profile. Maybe I wasn't clear."

He was lying, for sure. I knew it and he knew I knew it. Our eyes met and he turned into the house.

"I'll go," I stammered. My embarrassment was mounting toward mortification. Not only had I infuriated him enough to fire me, but now I had cornered him into lying about it. "Uh, sorry. You don't have to—"

"Michael." His voice was soft, stern. "Come in."

I fidgeted on the couch while he moved around the kitchen. The main area of the house was open—the sitting room, with the TV and fireplace, letting in to the kitchen. A loft overlooked both rooms. *Silence* was my first and most oppressive impression of the place. I wanted to clear my throat just to make a sound.

It didn't seem to bother him, though. For a long time, he prepared his breakfast without looking at me or addressing me. He brewed a pot of coffee and rummaged through the fridge. He took out a few pieces of fruit, washed and sliced them.

The sight of him wielding a large knife made me uneasy, and then I wanted to laugh. Somehow, he noticed.

"What?" he said.

"Hm? Nothing." I sprawled my legs across the carpet, striving for a comfortable appearance. His gaze was searing.

"You were smiling."

"Oh, just thinking."

"About what?" He moved the fruit to a plate.

About you going all The Shining *on me. Here's Johnny!* "Seriously, nothing."

"Tell me."

I puffed out a breath. There was no getting around it. I had to build trust with him, and what better way than by telling the truth? "It's weird, but I was laughing because"—I gestured airily—"you with that knife, for a moment, I thought, what if he's upset I showed up?" I laughed a little.

He frowned and slid the knife into its holder. "That's dark."

"Yeah. My mind, it's weird like that."

"I read your blog." He brought the fruit over and set it on the coffee table. He definitely tensed as he neared me, and he took a wedge of pear and retreated immediately.

"Oh." He had researched me. "Is that how you found my stream?"

"Yeah. What was that, exactly? I was confused." He moved to a spot between the couch and kitchen and paced restively, sipping his coffee and eating the fruit. Today, he looked a shade better than he had on Friday. His skin was pale, but not ashen, and his long hair was confined to a ponytail at the nape of his neck. He was the kind of guy who could get away with that, the kind of guy my girlfriend would have drooled over.

A first line for the profile flitted through my thoughts— *Caleb Bright is literally tall, dark, and handsome . . . no homo*—and I smirked again.

"What?" He had stopped moving and was staring at me intently.

"The stream." I shrank. "That's my thing. I mean, my job. Wow, you have to forgive me. I swear, I'm not always this . . ." Words fled my brain, the traitors.

"Ineloquent?" he supplied. "I know. Like I said, I read your blog. I'm confident in your ability to spin all this silly grinning into coherent sentences. On paper, at least." He padded back over, retrieved another piece of fruit, and returned to a safe distance. "Help yourself, by the way. Coffee?"

Coffee sounded good, and possibly it would get my neurons firing, but it might also spin me further into anxiety. "No, thank you," I said. Sooner rather than later, I needed to overcome this powerful feeling of inadequacy in his presence. I felt less-than, and it wasn't his doing. Not today, anyway. On Friday, he had deliberately made me feel like dog shit with his interrogation about my journalism experience, his sneering response to my gaming question, and his withering glare.

Today, though, he was mostly polite and curious. I didn't mind his occasional sarcasm and cynicism. I sensed that was part of his fear, like the distance he put between us. But I would never be able to write about him if I couldn't meet him on level ground. I made myself take a piece of apple and munched it down before explaining my stream. The more I described, the more baffled he became.

"So people pay to watch you play video games?"

"Computer games," I said.

"Sure." He waved a hand. "Still. That's crazy."

"It's a community. I'm there all week. We have a common interest . . . and they like my personality. That's a big part of it, personality."

"You are funny," he admitted.

"I guess. I'm just myself, but you definitely build a personal brand as you go. There are tons of trolls. They—"

"Trolls?"

"Oh. Like, jerks. Assholes. Basically people who are there to be rude in the chat, or start arguments. It's kind of fifty percent trolls, fifty percent people looking for a sense of belonging. I cater to both. I mean, they're all boosting my view count."

He smiled thinly. "Clever."

"It's good business."

"Yeah. Very interesting." He chewed and nodded. "A whole subsection of the Internet that I didn't know existed." He kept returning for fruit and then wandering away. He must not have realized or cared how pathological that seemed. Nearly any other person would have taken a seat, talked to me and looked at me.

Without expression, his face fell into a resting appearance of unhappiness. It wasn't quite a frown, but it was the face of someone permanently tired or troubled. I tracked him to and fro; I looked away when he glared at me, as if warning me off staring.

Not for the first time, I conceived of him as a cornered animal. *People who feel anxious act mean.* Hadn't I said those exact words to myself on my first drive up here? And maybe my thoughts had been silly then, the way I had envisioned approaching with hands up and earning his trust, but they seemed very practical now.

"I really can't take that money." I bit a piece of pear. It dissolved into sugary juice on my tongue, just like the apple had, and I groaned. "This fruit is—"

"What's wrong with it?" he snapped.

I almost coughed out the bite of pear. He had come to a rigid standstill and he was scowling at me, his face contorted with frustration. Or maybe it was rage.

"No, n-nothing. It's good. That's what I was—"

"Finish it then. I'm going to smoke."

He stalked out, slamming the deck door. I deflated. The whole house seemed to relax in his wake. "What in the actual fuck?" I whispered.

Methodically, because I was afraid of what might happen to his mood if I didn't, I polished off the last six slices of fruit. I didn't move from the couch. I looked toward the deck once; he was standing stiffly at the railing, his back to me, plumes of smoke expanding in the cold air.

I wouldn't have minded standing out there with him, vicariously enjoying the cigarette and looking over the lake, but that seemed out of the question. Both times he had exited to the deck in my presence, he had done so in a way that said, "I'm considering killing you with this sliding door." I exhaled and let myself smile. I had to find the humor in this bizarre situation; confusion would overwhelm me otherwise.

I floated theories as he smoked another cigarette.

He had an obvious Dr. Jekyll and Mr. Hyde thing going on, which made me wonder if he suffered from a mood disorder—bipolar, maybe, or antisocial.

I tried to find some link between the fruit and my fall on his walkway. Had he thought I was choking on the pear? Was he worried that I might try to take advantage of him by way of a lawsuit? Fears like that plagued the wealthy, I knew, and he was clearly wealthy. Everything in his home was elegant, understated, and yet noticeably top drawer. Marble countertops and sturdy, stainless steel appliances gleamed in the kitchen. The table there was solid, rustic in design. The couches, armchairs, pillows, and throws were all suede and sheepskin, heavily stitched, in taupe and mocha shades. And the rooms themselves were immaculately clean, but comfortable, lived-in.

He stepped back inside and closed the door circumspectly. He even looked a little chagrined. I sat up straighter and smiled. "I was thinking—"

"I get the fruit at a farmers' market." He spoke right over me. "Local farmers' market. It's great, isn't it? I'll take you some time, if you want. It ends early next month." He strolled over purposefully, took the fruit plate, and carried it to the sink. "Don't mention the money. Really, after your face, and the laptop—"

"Well, while we're on that topic—"

"How is your face, by the way?" He scrubbed the plate with religious zeal. I swear, I pitied the plate.

"It's fine. It was a shallow cut." I was lying through my teeth, but I'd be damned if I told him how the gash had crusted over the weekend, then broken open and oozed gummy yellow fluid. I had doused it with rubbing alcohol, packed it with Neosporin and gauze, and sealed it under a fat bandage.

"Was it?" He paused and looked at me. Either he saw the lie on my face or the suspiciously bulky dressing.

"My girlfriend is a pharmacist. She's neurotic about infection." I pointed to the bandaging. "She goes overboard." More lies. I was hiding the wound from Nicole as much as I was hiding it from Cal, because I didn't want her to pester me about a doctor visit. And she would, if she saw the thing.

"I see." He resumed the aggressive scrubbing. There couldn't have been a trace of fruit DNA left on the plate—and then he put it in the dishwasher. I rubbed my mouth. Laughing now would be inappropriate, for sure.

"Look, I wanted you to know, I would be happy to sign any kind of document you drew up . . . if you have concerns."

I couldn't decide which was worse, the fanatical door slamming and plate scrubbing or this steady, impenetrable stare.

"Concerns?" he said.

"Anything, you know." I waved a hand. "Privacy concerns, legal concerns. Anything you want kept out of the profile. Anything." *Oh, please, why can't I stop saying anything?* "Anything at all that would make this easier. I would be happy to sign any—"

"Sure." He raised a hand, putting me out of my misery. "I appreciate that."

I sagged into the couch. Suddenly, I knew what his home needed: A dog, a cat, a plant, any other living thing for me to watch. *Anything.* There was an airless quality to the place with just the two of us in there, and it was keying me up to peak anxiety.

"That deck looks amazing." I launched myself off the couch and made a break for it. I had to get some air, and there would be trees to look at outside, and wind and sound.

He strained into the corner of the counter, blinking at me. What was wrong with this guy? "The deck?"

"Yeah, the view. Do you mind?" My hand was on the door.

"No. No, go on. Walk around. I have to make a call." He headed in the other direction, moving deeper into the house, and I was just as glad that he did.

7

CALEB

Mistakes were made. Maybe the first mistake had been calling my ex-wife on Friday night, or, even before that, opening the door to Michael Beck. Circumstances had forced my hand, though. He had fallen, broken his laptop. I couldn't have left him lying there.

Contrary to what I was sure he thought, I'm not a monster.

But Googling him, reading his blog, watching his stream, and giving him two thousand dollars—those were clear-cut mistakes. And when he had reappeared today, looking so puffed up with anger and embarrassment, and trying to return my money, I had agreed to let him write the profile. That was a mistake, too.

Calling my ex-wife, though—I saw that for what it was. I was giving myself permission to reopen the door to Michael Beck, because I didn't have anything else left in my life. I didn't have a relationship with my son. I didn't have a career. I only had my parents and sister, and they weren't enough these days. Not nearly.

I sat in my office, waiting out the time I supposed it would take to make a call. Really, I needed a few moments away from Michael. But then, after a minute, I realized I did have a call to make.

Beth answered promptly. "Cal?" She sounded upbeat. She probably hadn't expected to hear from me after my furious voicemail about the journalist.

"Beth, hi."

"Great to hear from you. What's going on?"

"Oh, it's about the profile, you know—"

"Perfect. I'm glad you mentioned it. The magazine *just* emailed me a new list of journalists. Your pick, Cal. Can I forward it over? Don't give up on this."

"That's the thing." I drummed my fingers on the desk. I wasn't at all embarrassed to be changing my mind. I liked surprising Beth (and stressing her out a little). It wasn't fair for the stress to flow in only one direction. "I want that Michael Beck kid."

"Come again?"

I licked my lips. "The journalist from Friday, the one from Colorado."

"Yes. I talked to the editor. You won't ever have to—"

"No, I *want* him on the profile, Beth. No one else. Let the magazine know, will you please? Let them know there was a misunderstanding."

I smiled miserably at the ensuing silence. How sad, to get my kicks like this.

"That . . . works. Okay. Michael . . . Beck." She was typing aggressively. "Perfect. I'll call the magazine now."

"Good. Thank you."

"Let's not change things again, okay?" She switched to her serious tone. "We could lose their interest, or come off as—"

"No more changes. I'm not that fickle."

"Great. Good. Happy to hear this, Cal. Keep in touch."

"Will do." I ended the call and left the office.

What I had told her was true: I wasn't fickle.

Barefoot, I strolled across the deck and searched my property for Michael. Maybe he had done the smart thing and headed for the hills—but no, there he was, stumbling through the tall grass on the southern edge of the lake. He did not belong in nature. Not yet, anyway. I would have to see what I could do about that.

The wind rolling down the mountains dragged his hair across his face and tore at his coat. Today, he had opted for a plain black hoodie, probably because his game T-shirt had gone over like a lead balloon. The poor guy; he must have felt like he couldn't win with me. And I had been cruel to him on Friday. Even today, I knew I was behaving strangely. I needed time to get used to his presence.

He caught sight of me and swerved toward the deck.

I motioned for him to stay by the lake. "I'll come down," I called. Maybe things would be easier outdoors. I ducked inside, stuffed my feet into unlaced boots, and pulled on a wool coat. For whatever reason, Michael seemed to like dressing half his age, though it didn't look bad. The quirky style suited him.

I strolled down the rocky slope to the lake.

"This place is beautiful," he said, squinting against the wind.

"I agree." I kept my distance, picking a path beside the water. A cigarette would make a good excuse to stay away from him, so I lit one.

"How long have you smoked?" He tried to walk with me. I forged ahead, my longer legs and surer footing outpacing him easily.

"Four years, give or take."

"Ever since you moved here, then?"

He had done his homework, apparently. "Yes, that's right. I'm guessing you know I have a son."

"Uh, I do, yeah. Sorry, I—"

"Well, I wasn't about to smoke around him."

"No. That makes sense. Sorry." He had embarrassed himself by admitting to researching me. That was part of his job, but he was too much of a novice to own it. I filed away that information. The fact that he wasn't a seasoned journalist worked in my favor. It would make him easier to handle.

"Does it bother you?" I gestured with the cigarette.

"Not at all. I like the smell. They'll kill you, though."

"I don't mind." I smirked. "I know where I'm going."

"You're . . . pretty spiritual, right?"

I turned back toward the house. Outside, I was fast realizing, I had two choices: Charge ahead of him while he scrutinized my every move (I could feel his eyes on me) or slow down and let him walk beside me, which was too close for comfort. Inside, at least, I could install him on the couch and go wherever I wanted.

"If, by 'pretty spiritual,' you mean a Christian, then yes."

"That's interesting." He continued trying to catch up, even on the hill. I heard him puffing behind me, his coat rustling furiously.

"Not as interesting as you might think."

"Well, you don't meet many"—he inhaled raggedly—"fundamental Christians nowadays, or people who subscribe to one particular—"

"Don't overexert yourself, Michael." I rounded on the deck stairs. I wanted to laugh, but that would have been rude.

"I'm fine." He flashed a beleaguered smile and trudged up to the railing.

"You don't work out," I recited, "you level up."

"Exactly." He sagged against the house. "Do you work out?"

His nonstop questions were not unlike his efforts to keep up with me: Futile, pitiful, overeager, and obvious. "Look," I said, "let's not get into everything today, okay?" I kicked off my boots and shed my coat on the kitchen table. He made a beeline for the couch. I brought him a glass of water, which he sucked down in several swallows. "You have two months to work on the article, right?"

He nodded, struggling out of his jacket.

"That's a long time. You don't even have your materials today."

"True. Yeah."

"So, let's figure out a schedule and exchange contact info and call it a day." I dropped a pen and notepad on the coffee table and walked away.

8

MICHAEL

"You're going up there three times a week?" Nicole took her breakfast dishes to the sink. Furio trailed her, his tuft of a tail waving hopefully. "Don't you think that's a lot?"

"I'm not sure it's enough, honestly." I had my new MacBook open on the table and I was transferring Cal's schedule to the calendar. I had been able to recover the files from my old laptop, but the machine itself was dead, the first casualty in my siege on Fort Bright. "I have to really get to know this guy. He has to feel comfortable around me. And right now, he's . . ." I shook my head. No one word could explain, and if I started rethinking my second encounter with the author, I would be lost in a spiral of theories.

"Crazy, right? You were sure he was gonna cancel the thing last Friday. Now he wants to meet three times a week?"

I hadn't told Nicole that Cal actually had cancelled the profile, only to do a one-eighty after I tried to return his money. I hadn't told her about the donation, either, and she wasn't happy that I had splurged on a laptop without running it by her first.

Everything came down to money for Nicole, which was strange, considering I was broke when we met. And sure, she had helped transform me into a successful almost-adult, but the bulk of that initiative had involved warping my hobbies into business models. My love of gaming had become streaming. The pleasure I got out of making people laugh had become blogging. My self-deprecating humor was now a selling point, and my funny-witty thoughts only had value insofar as they generated readers.

Nicole wasn't done with me, either. She nettled at me patiently, relentlessly, making her wishes known. Sentences I heard on the regular included: *Is that what you're wearing? You should start walking Furio; it would be good for both of you. Wow, that guy is incredibly fit. Do you know what's in that? I wish we could do Bolder Boulder together, but you would literally die.*

In Nicole's ideal universe, I would reach my final form when I lived in preppy, fair-trade clothing, eschewed chemical products and processed foods in favor of organic alternatives, and woke at 5 AM for my daily run/cycle/swim.

And sometimes, just sometimes, I began to see her vision. The pressure of her wishes became an impetus, and I wondered if I could form myself into that man.

"Mike?"

"Huh?"

"I said, what about the stream?"

"What about the stream?"

"With this interview schedule, you'll definitely lose subscribers."

"I lose subs every day. That's how it works. It goes up and down."

"What's the count at now? It must be pretty high, if you felt comfortable buying that thing. How much was it again?"

She meant the laptop, which I had tricked out with a solid-state hard drive and top-of-the-line processor, and which had come to just under two thousand dollars. And Nicole and I had been over that, twice.

"Still hovering around three thousand subs. I'll adjust the stream schedule; it'll be fine. And this is a tax write-off, remember? It's a work expense."

"I know, I know. But streaming is your *real* work. Journalism—"

"Are we going to argue about this?" I lifted my laptop and coffee. I was trying so hard to find the humor in the situation, and failing. Nicole knew that *The New Yorker* was a big deal. She knew I wanted to do journalism for a living. She just didn't care.

"We're not arguing." She pouted. "We're talking."

"Either way, I need to go."

"Me too. Don't be upset." She gave me a peck on the mouth.

"I'm not," I lied. "Don't forget Furio today."

"I won't. I love you."

"Love you," I said automatically.

That day, Nicole would have to drive home on her lunch break and feed Furio because I would be in Red Feather. Cal and I had decided to meet on Mondays, Wednesdays, and Fridays, with the occasional weekend get-together. At least once, I wanted to attend church with him. The farmers' market, too. And whatever else he did.

I would learn about him by osmosis, observation, and conversation. I had drawn a tree of topics (writing/art, family/friends, faith/upbringing, future goals) and I intended to fill it out with an emphasis on his interior, creative life.

But first, he and I had some basics to resolve, like eye contact, standing within less than three yards of one another, and not feeling so damn intimidated.

That last point, though, was more my problem than his.

9

CALEB

MICHAEL, IN HIS INFINITE WISDOM, had decided to shadow me one day per week. He would alternate Mondays, Wednesdays, and Fridays. Today was Monday. What was I getting myself into? It was too late to change my mind, but I shouldn't have agreed to the all-day thing, I really shouldn't have.

He arrived at ten and knocked.

"You can start letting yourself in," I said, twisting away from the door. My eyes strafed over him, fast enough to see that his hair was still damp from a shower and he was wearing his usual jacket/hoodie/jeans combo. He had overdone it with the cologne and I didn't want to smell his cologne *or* his shampoo and I could smell both.

"Sure. Whatever works for you."

"You letting yourself in works." I sat and finished tying my shoes. He plopped onto the couch beside me and I jumped up. He stood, too. I moved into the kitchen.

"So, what's up for today?"

"Well, I'm going to run"—I gestured to my attire: A long-sleeved Under Armour shirt, sweats, and trail running sneakers—"as you can possibly tell."

"You do work out, then."

"Clearly." I turned away. I was pissed at myself for letting him into my life—for crumbling impulsively, for being so weak—and that anger was emerging in my every word and move. He didn't deserve that, but I couldn't seem to pull it back.

"Do you mind if I come with?"

I snorted. "You must be kidding."

"No, I . . . one sec." I heard him retreating and when I glanced back, he was removing layers of clothing.

"What the hell are you doing?" I was sure I looked as appalled as I felt. He lifted off his hoodie and exposed a slice of pale stomach, and the waistband of black boxers, before tugging down his T-shirt. I glared out at the lake.

"I'll go part of the way with you. I figure this will be fine." He meant the T-shirt and jeans, I guessed, and the sneakers with less than zero arch support. Was there an opposite of support? Was there footwear that did actual, quantifiable harm to the wearer's feet? Because Michael's shoes had that look.

"No offense, but—"

"Cal, I'll be fine. I want to immerse myself in your routine, okay?" He laughed. "That sounds weird, but you get what I mean."

I rubbed my face. "Fine. Don't blame me if you end up in the ER."

The morning was cold and clear. I did a few stretches on the deck and Michael attempted to replicate them. I ignored him.

"You do this every day?" he said.

"Yeah."

"How does that work with smoking?"

"Works fine."

"Do you normally get up earlier than this? I don't want to mess with your—"

"No. I'm not an early riser." I bounded down the steps.

"Sweet. So how far do you—"

I took off running. I left Michael in the dust, literally, with his damp hair that smelled like leaves and his infuriating cologne and his idiotic questions. I hoped he tripped and fell in the fucking lake.

As for me, I went wide around it, into the trees where I'd made a trail, up the hill and back, finishing the circuit with a lap around the lake. *This* is how far I run, Michael.

10

MICHAEL

I NEEDED A NAME FOR Angry Cal. Angry Cal was back. He didn't want to jog with me; he didn't want me at his house. I flailed after him as he sprinted into the trees. Sweat popped out of my brow immediately, in spite of the cold, and my heart juddered.

"Wow!" I called toward his retreating figure. I wanted to add something to the effect of "don't worry about me" or "go ahead and do your usual thing," but my powers of speech had already dissolved into panting. Besides, he was clearly not worried about me, and he was clearly doing his usual thing, just as he was *clearly* jogging on account of his outfit and *clearly* worked out.

"Clearly," I mumbled, dropping onto the deck stairs. Sweat streaked down the sides of my face. I hadn't even reached the trees before turning back.

Cal was right; I would have ended up in the ER if I had tried to keep up. Maybe that's what had ticked him off today—the fact that I had arrived before his morning run and then insisted on accompanying him. Was that insensitive?

"No," I told myself sharply. I kicked a rock as hard as I could. It rolled a pathetically short distance. No, my attempt to run with him was *not* insensitive. He was fucking insensitive, tearing off like that. He must have been on his fucking period today. "You letting yourself in works," I mimicked him in an unflattering voice. "I *clearly* work out; look at my biceps in this skin-tight shirt."

I yammered away like that for a good five minutes.

It didn't help.

Then I waited, because going inside without him felt invasive.

I cooled off quickly and soon I was shivering. Gooseflesh prickled beneath the sweat on my face and arms, which made me even colder. A constant breeze seemed to come off the mountains, over the lake. My teeth chattered and I hugged myself and thought hard about darting in to grab my jacket.

But it would be just my luck that he would return as I was going in and then he'd accuse me of snooping or theft or God knew what went through his demented head.

Sure enough, he rounded the bend of the lake at that moment.

"Relax," I told myself. "This is your job. He's a job." And again, I felt a jag of pity, because something was obviously wrong with him.

I pasted on a cheerful smile as he jogged toward the house. I stood and waved.

His expression remained grim as he slowed to a walk and climbed the hill. Sweat shone on his face. His mouth hung open and his powerful shoulders rose and fell with deep, heavy breaths.

"Dude, nice job," I said as he stalked past. I gave him a slap on the back. I felt him tense before my hand had even left his spine. He turned swiftly and slammed me into the side of the house. The shock of it hurt more than the actual collision. I gasped and covered my head, ducking, ready for a blow. My ears were ringing, my pulse roaring.

When I finally cracked open my eyes, he was gone.

The deck door stood open, cold air invading the kitchen. I held my breath as I stepped inside. One glance around the main room confirmed he wasn't there, and then I heard the faint rushing sound of a shower.

I grabbed my hoodie, coat, and laptop, hurried to my car, and peeled out of the drive, because to hell with that guy and to hell with that job.

11

CALEB

It was bad, after I shoved Michael. It was the worst it had been in a long time. It reminded me of that first night with Jamie.

I took my knife to the bathroom, locked the door, and turned on the shower. I stripped and stepped under the boiling water. My mind was speeding, speeding like an unmanned train, flashing faster and faster and faster.

I carved into my inner thigh.

Ribbons of blood maypoled my leg, feathering into the dark hairs, spiraling pink around and down the drain.

12

MICHAEL

THERE ARE A FEW DEPRESSING little towns between Red Feather and I-25, and I got stalled in one of them on my way down from the mountains. There must have been an accident up ahead; the main street of that town would never see so much traffic otherwise.

I eased the Jeep to a standstill behind an interminable line of cars. Nobody was honking yet or climbing out to try to get a look at the situation.

Nobody had anywhere to go, me least of all.

My heart had finally thudded back to its steady, innocuous rhythm. My fingers relaxed around the wheel and my thighs and arms unclenched.

I had been, until that point, in full fight-or-flight mode. More flight than fight, to be fair, but my body was ready for anything.

I swallowed and my saliva tasted bitter.

He had actually attacked me. It had happened so fast that I couldn't be sure if I was remembering it right or inflating it in my mind, but he had definitely shoved me into the side of the house. I had simply patted his back and he had snapped.

I remembered the look I had seen on his face the first time I laid eyes on him, after I fell on his walkway: A look of violence, a look of barely contained revulsion.

"What is wrong with you?" I said aloud.

Out the window to my left was a liquor store, a staple in towns like that, and to the right was a faux Native American gift shop. Cowboy hats, geodes, belt buckles, pipes, and little wooden carvings filled the front display. *What a culture clash*, I thought absently, and I felt depressed and dark.

Where was I going?

Was I going home to sit in my basement office and stream computer games?

The image of my office seemed as sad and small as that gift shop, as that town. I felt that I was giving up, which wasn't in my nature, and something more—something almost indescribable. When I was in a room with that insane author, I felt alive. Anything could happen. He could attack me, or I could end up running around a lake, wheezing and sweating. What if I could make him laugh? What if he could explain to me what was going on in his brain? He was strange and spectacular, like no one I had ever met. I didn't want to go away from that. I didn't want a safe and boring life.

I pulled out of the static line of cars and U-turned, back toward the mountains.

13

CALEB

When I heard tires on the drive, my first thought was that Michael had called the cops before high-tailing it back to Boulder, which would have served me right. He wasn't Jamie; we weren't teenagers. We were grown men and I had assaulted him.

Whatever the case, I remained seated at the kitchen table, one hand cradling a glass of whiskey. I had a reasonable buzz going, enough to numb my mind so that my thoughts tumbled along softly instead of cutting up my brain with their clarity.

Michael let himself in, which actually caused me to smirk.

"It's me," he said carefully, though I could very well see him on the periphery of my vision. "Figured I could . . . let myself in." He chuckled half-heartedly. He saw the humor in it, too.

"A learning machine," I mumbled.

"That's me." He edged his way into the kitchen. For the second time that month, but more seriously now, I wondered if I was going insane. It made no sense for Michael to have returned. Only in my imaginings would this person come back.

I spent a lot of time alone in my house. Too much time, maybe. Was it possible that I had conjured up the entire thing—the profile, the journalist, these visits? But I had talked to my agent. I had talked to my ex-wife. Or could my mind produce something that elaborate? I supposed I shouldn't put anything past it, my mind.

"Do you mind if I sit?" He was standing at a safe distance.

I gestured to the chair across from mine, at the far end of the table. He sat, opened his laptop. I watched without looking directly at him. I was preoccupied, and embarrassed.

"That new?" I said after a while.

"Yeah. Brand new MacBook Pro. Sixteen gigs of memory, i7 processor, retina display, SSD—you name it."

"The works."

"The *whole* works." He sounded happy, but he cringed as I pushed away from the table and wandered past. I retrieved a glass and set it near him. I slid the bottle of whiskey over and retook my seat.

"Oh. Thanks." He poured himself a modest amount and sipped it. "Good stuff."

I drained my glass in agreement.

For a while then, we sat in a semi-comfortable silence. Wind pressed against the house. He scooted the whiskey toward me. I poured myself another two fingers and slid the bottle back. He drank, typed, refilled his glass. I informed him that my Wi-Fi had no password, seeing as no one lived close enough to take advantage of it.

"So have at it," I said. I was still staring at the table, feeling pleasantly lightheaded. A damp spot crept along my inner thigh, as if blood were leaking through the gauze and medical tape I had put there. No matter. After my shower, I had changed into a sweater and black jeans, just in case.

"You might regret saying that. I can eat up a lot of bandwidth."

I smiled faintly.

More silence, more wind and branches scraping against the house, and then he cleared his throat. "Can I ask you something?" He had made his voice as soft, as unobtrusive as possible. It could almost have been the wind.

I nodded a little.

He moved his glass slowly from hand to hand, the heavy base dragging against the grain of the table. I liked the noise. I was calm, almost sleepy.

"Did something . . . happen to you?"

I could have played dumb, but I knew what he meant, and he deserved some answers after coming back. The more I reflected on the fact that he had come back, the more supernatural it seemed. I was glad, though, so glad he had.

"Not in the way you're thinking," I said, because I knew he was imagining that I had been abused. That would rationalize my jumpiness, my outburst. "I had a good childhood. Practically perfect. My parents never did any wrong by me. I've lied about other things, and I'm sure I'll lie again, but about this, I'm telling the truth."

"What is it, then?" He leaned forward.

I shook my head and he let it go.

But I was in the mood for conversation, surprisingly, so I asked how he could stand living in cramped Boulder with all its hippies and vegans and he told me about his life there, his girlfriend and corgi.

"Furio? Is he furious?"

"Not at all." He laughed. "It's from *The Sopranos*. My favorite character."

I admitted I had never seen the show and he insisted that I should.

"I would re-watch it with you," he said. "Seriously." Two shallow glasses of whiskey and his face was already flushed and he wanted to marathon a television show with me. That made me think about how easy it would be for someone to take advantage of him, which made me angry.

"Like I said"—I gestured toward the TV with my drink—"have at it."

I went out to smoke while he logged in to his HBO account on my TV. He was still fiddling with it when I came back in.

"I can't get over the smoking and running," he said.

"The eternal mystery." I brought the whiskey to the family room and refilled both our glasses.

"What's the motivation for working out?"

"Isn't it obvious?" I slouched into the corner of the couch, closed my eyes, and propped my feet on the coffee table. "If it's not health, and it's not health, it's vanity."

"Oh."

I laughed a little, low in my throat. What a child he was.

Out of fear or respect for my space, he sat at the opposite end of the couch. We would have looked slightly ridiculous to anyone else.

I watched the show and he half-watched while working on his laptop.

"By the way, thank you," he blurted out at one point.

Whatever he was thanking me for, I waved it away.

14

MICHAEL

It was difficult to stop drinking Cal's good whiskey and sober up for the drive home. He had no reason to stop, though, and drank into the evening. He seemed to enjoy *The Sopranos*, chuckling from time to time.

But then, around eight, he capped the whiskey and stood, frowning severely.

"You should go," he said.

I hustled, jamming my laptop into its case and grabbing my coat. He wouldn't look at me, though that was no different than usual.

"Are you good to drive?" he asked belatedly.

"Definitely. I had my last drink four episodes ago."

"Are you sure? I could get you a taxi, call a hotel." His voice barely betrayed the amount of alcohol I had watched him consume over the last few hours.

A taxi, a hotel . . . passing out on his couch was not an option, apparently. Maybe he turned into a wolf at night.

I grinned on my way to the door and he caught me grinning.

"What?" he said.

For someone who barely looked my way, he missed very little.

I answered without hesitation, my expression somber. "I was thinking about how obvious it is that you're a werewolf."

He didn't miss a beat. "Is it really that obvious?"

"Blatant, I'm afraid. And yes, I'm sure. No worries."

"Pull over if you get tired."

That was easily the most thoughtful thing he had said to me to date and I took a half-second to appreciate it before opening the door. "I will. Feel free to use that HBO account any time, by the way. My password should stay in there."

I headed out quickly, before things could go south.

I decided I had made the right choice in returning to Red Feather, even though I had been afraid. Anyone in his right mind would have warned me against it, but I didn't care.

Besides, I could always claim that I had gone back for *The New Yorker*, for the job, the opportunity. But that wouldn't make it true. I had gone back for him and it had paid off. We had finally established a twisted sort of association—not quite a friendship, but more than an acquaintance—and I didn't care that the breakthrough had involved him shoving me into a wall. I really didn't care.

Tuesday was almost intolerable. I posted a new stream schedule on my social media (extended hours on Tuesdays and Thursdays, bonus streams on the weekends) and then I streamed from eight in the morning until six in the evening. It was a grueling marathon. My butt went numb, even in my DXRacer gaming chair, and that's saying something. I cycled through four games. I was peevish and exhausted by six.

I wondered, more than once, if Cal was watching. He had a right to, in a sense. I was watching his life, looking into his background.

On Wednesday, I made sure to show up at his house after his morning run.

I must have nailed the timing. When I let myself in, he was standing in the kitchen, watching the coffee pot expectantly. His hair was wet, loose. He wore black on black, again, like he lived in a state of mourning.

He didn't even look my way. The author in his natural habitat. I kept my eyes down and headed to the couch. My lips twitched; I rubbed at them, as if that could satisfy the laughter tickling my throat. Helplessly, I was imagining the scene as something off Animal Planet: Tribal music in the background, Cal staring at the coffee pot, me creeping into the house, some British dude narrating. *The journalist keeps his head lowered in a display of submission. The author will only acknowledge the lesser male if—*

"What is it now?" he said.

I jumped. "Morning."

"What's so funny?"

I thought briefly about trying to articulate the image and then lifted my hands in surrender. "Please, don't make me explain this one."

With a dramatic *sching*, he unsheathed a vegetable knife from the holder. "Don't make me use this." His expression was so stoic that it took me a moment to process the joke. Then I laughed irrepressibly, partly at him, partly at my own thoughts, and mostly out of relief. He was in a decent mood.

"Okay, uh, when I came in here just now, I . . ." I laughed again, pinching the bridge of my nose. "Cal, these things are funnier in my head."

"No, they are definitely funnier when you try to explain them."

I sighed and shook my head. "Okay, in my head, it was like, a nature program. You know, with the jazzy jungle music in the background and some guy narrating?"

He gave me a long, dry stare. "Go on."

"Cause you were just chilling over there and I was all"—I gestured vaguely, my face warming—"trying to keep a low profile, skulking in."

He poured himself a cup of coffee and moved to the deck door. I thought he might go out to smoke and leave me alone in my weirdness, but he spoke up after a beat. "If we were both predators, I would have taken you out a long time ago."

"Exactly." I grinned. He got it.

"Maybe I wouldn't even have to," he continued thoughtfully. "You'd be that lion that just takes himself out. Runs off a cliff by accident." He was alluding, I assumed, to my fall on his walkway. I shook with laughter.

"Low blow, dude."

"How is your cut, by the way?"

"To be honest, it wasn't looking so hot for a while, but—"

He appeared suddenly, striding around the couch. "You said it was fine on Monday. Just a scratch."

"Well, I didn't want to worry you, and now it—"

"Do *not* lie to me," he snapped. "Let me see it."

I had a regular bandage over the wound that day and the gash was finally healing. The pink, inflamed skin around it had returned to a normal tone and the crusting and oozing had cleared. Cal loomed like he was about to rip off the bandage himself, though, so I peeled it down gently.

He had never, of his own volition, stood so close to me. He seized my jaw and tilted my face to get a better look. I held perfectly still, my eyes round. It wasn't like the shove—this gesture came from a place of concern—but it still startled me.

He glared at the wound while I thanked my stars that I hadn't lied and that it was, in fact, better. At last, he made a quiet, dismissive sound and released me.

"Don't lie to me again," he said.

Then he left, storming out to the deck, while I wondered if I had ruined his mood.

I hadn't, it seemed. He returned from smoking and began talking at me and pacing around the kitchen. "I got out these albums for you. They're family photos and things. Come look at them."

I brought my laptop to the kitchen table, where he had piled four large photo albums. "Oh, wow." This was about as surprising as the face-grab. Given our first two meetings, I had thought I would need to pry every piece of information out of his mouth. "This is great." I opened the first album.

"Everything is labeled. It's mostly my parents, my sister and I, some cousins and aunts and uncles. Grandparents, too. The grandparents have all passed away."

He lectured me on his upbringing in Massachusetts, which he claimed had been happy and ordinary, and his family's history. His grandparents, staunch evangelical Christians, had left England and New Zealand as missionaries to Brazil. They had planted churches and raised their families there, and one of his uncles still continued the work.

"He runs a large Bible conference every year. It's in the jungle, the interior. One phone booth, no Internet. Thousands of people go to hear the speakers. It's amazing."

"You've been?" I typed frantically, taking notes as fast as I could.

"Oh, yes. Several times. The messages are in Portuguese, but I understand enough to get by. What I really love is the place. The heat, the rain, the trees. There are wild macaws, coral snakes, monkeys. It's like something out of a movie."

"You like . . . nature," I observed carefully. "Remote areas."

He stopped pacing and glowered at me. "Please, rise above the Caleb Bright is a Salinger-esque recluse thing."

I laughed. "I wasn't going to go there, don't worry."

"Good. I'm not a writer anymore. I'm not publishing. I'm just a man with a house in the mountains, like anyone else living out here. The reclusive writer thing is played out and it's silly." He resumed pacing, describing how his parents had moved to

America, his birthplace and his sister's, his father's work (surgery) and his mother's (homemaking). It was all almost uncomfortably traditional. They had been a churchgoing family for generations and still were. Even the surly man before me, who smoked and drank and occasionally swore, apparently went to church each Sunday.

That, I had to see.

His parents lived in Cambridge and Martha's Vineyard. His sister was married and had two small boys. She visited him often and he saw his parents each summer. "My family is everything to me," he said. "My family and my faith." I didn't doubt him, though the lines sounded curiously rehearsed.

Growing up, he had attended and eventually volunteered at a Christian camp in Pennsylvania. He had excelled in school—no surprise there—and attended Harvard.

My eyes glazed over a little as I listened. I was picturing it: The clean living, the privilege, the charitable work, and summers at the beach.

"I was a lifeguard for a while," he said, "at the camp and a pool near home."

"Of course you were." The words slipped out from my interior monologue. He halted again and frowned at me.

"What do you mean, of course I was?"

I had meant, in my private thoughts, that he struck me as the type of guy who was never not fit. He had probably started working out in high school and continued to this very day. His teeth were electrically white and surgically straight. He cut an imposing figure. He spoke a second language. He had an Ivy League education under his belt *and* the luxury of doing nothing with it, just having it there, an expensive accessory.

He was everything my girlfriend wanted me to be and then some. The real deal. The actual dream. I cleared my throat and gazed at one of the albums. The glossy stills of his family and friends confirmed everything he had said.

"I forget," I mumbled lamely.

"Tell me."

"Could I not?" I flipped a page. His sister had his tall, willowy figure, glossy black hair, and attractive face. She could have been a model. I turned the page again so as not to be caught staring at his sister in a bathing suit.

"Please," he said more gently. "I won't get upset. I'm curious."

"Ah, the lifeguarding just"—I pretended to be typing notes into my Word document (I typed: *wkw 3jkh3bkb rjthle*)—"seems, I mean, I can imagine . . ."

I glanced at him. One of his dark eyebrows was arched in almost comical anticipation of my next words. He was a good listener, I realized at once—a disconcertingly good listener. In fact, I couldn't bring to mind a single other person who stopped and stared at me the way he did when he asked me questions.

"Go on," he said.

"It's just that I can picture you lifeguarding, causing women everywhere to pretend to drown." I laughed.

"Ah." He nodded. He did not find that funny. His eyes narrowed. "At any rate, you look at those. I'll make some kind of lunch."

15

MICHAEL

Cal rattled around in the kitchen behind me. I smelled garlic and butter. Something sizzled while something else simmered.

It was infuriating, being unable to observe, but I think he had arranged it that way. He tended to put me where I couldn't watch him. The couch in the family room, for example, faced away from the kitchen and the deck. I had to peer over my shoulder to see him from there. And when he had invited me to look at the albums, he had pushed them in front of the chair that had its back to the stove and counters.

The clever bastard.

I wanted to smirk and shake my head, but he might somehow witness the gesture through the back of his head and demand to know what I was thinking. Then, if I didn't tell him, he would grab my face and order me never to lie to him.

Now it was a struggle, not laughing.

"Are you having fun over there?"

Sure enough, he had seen through my skull to my twitching face. Or maybe he had simply glimpsed my profile on his way to the pantry.

"Can we talk about your ex-wife?" I returned fire.

"Oh, I don't talk about any of that." He set an open bottle of beer near my elbow. It was exactly what I wanted, cold and hoppy and smooth.

"Thanks." I took another swallow. "Doesn't that seem a little unfair?"

"How so? You're writing for *The New Yorker*, not a tabloid." He was unruffled. His tone said: I can do this all day.

"I'm not looking for sensational stuff. But all this"—I touched the pile of albums—"is really ideal. Flaws, struggles, those are what make people real to us. It's disingenuous to leave that out, if only in terms of my mental picture."

"I see what you're saying."

More cooking noises sounded behind me. I would have moved to another chair, if I didn't honestly think he would have found a way to maneuver me back into this one.

"And?"

"And I'd be happy to talk about why I stopped writing, at some point. That was difficult. A struggle, as you put it." Again, the rehearsed tone. If he wasn't hiding something, he was at least glossing over it.

"What about your son?" I said.

"What about him?"

"Do you see him a lot?"

"Of course. Whenever I want. Ah, I have some of his things . . ." He crossed into the family room and disappeared into the office. Though he had never given me a tour of the house, I had used the bathroom on the main floor, I knew the door beside it led to the basement, and, passing the office, I had glimpsed a desk and bookshelves. I assumed his bedroom was in the loft.

He emerged carrying a stack of papers, which he set reverently in front of me. I moved my beer to the far side of the table.

"He's incredibly artistic. He did all of these," he said grandly. He hovered at my side, sliding one childish watercolor after another in front of me. He paused each time, letting me take them in, and it was obvious I was not to touch them.

"Caleb?" I eyed the crude signature.

"That's right. It's a southern thing." He waved a hand. "Anyway, he's Caleb and I'm Cal. He's doing this lately, just shades of green. He calls it his *personal style*. Five years old and he says, 'This is my personal style.'" He laughed.

Having displayed the last painting, he returned the sheaf to the office.

"Will I get to talk to them?" I said offhandedly.

"Sure, I'll put you in touch with my family. I'll give them a heads up and send you their info. My parents aren't big on technology, so give them a bit if you e-mail. And try not to overwhelm them with questions, you know?"

"Right, okay. What about your ex?"

"No, and she wouldn't comment anyway. You don't want to deal with her."

He placed a steaming plate onto the table beside me. He had made white pizza on two halves of French bread, flecks of garlic sinking into the ricotta and mozzarella. Of course, he said I should help myself while he cleaned up, and he drank his beer and ate his lunch at the counter behind me.

16

CALEB

RACHEL, MY SISTER, HAS A habit of dropping by unannounced. She has had this habit since we were children, and my teenage years (and the activities thereof) did not deter her. She would swing into my bedroom and holler, "Isn't this a pleasant surprise?" She coined the term "the pleasant surprise factor" and carried the habit into adulthood.

She would show up at camp in the boy's dormitory.

More than once, she snuck into my dorm room at Harvard.

When I was married and Rachel's arbitrary visits ticked off Coral, Rachel would pout and tell me that she couldn't give us more notice because it would ruin "the pleasant surprise factor." I never scolded her for it, of course.

I was becoming more intolerant to this behavior as I got older, though, when I think it should have been the other way around.

She appeared on my doorstep in the middle of October, sans children and husband. "I left everyone else in boring Massachusetts," she explained, hugging me tight and kissing my cheek. "Isn't this a pleasant surprise?" Her throaty voice tickled my ear. I lifted her off her feet and crushed her against my chest.

"Cal, your hair." She ran her fingers through the long pieces. They nearly touched the tops of my shoulders.

"I know. I need to get it cut." I gathered it back with a tie.

"No. I don't know." She smiled and clung to my arms, her dark eyes shining. "It's gorgeous. It's more beautiful than mine."

"No chance of that." I laughed. "I can't believe you're here." No matter how often she did this, it *was* a pleasant surprise. I walked out to her rental car and fetched her bag. It was small, light—just a carry-on. "One weekend?" I guessed.

"That's all I could manage. Kevin literally goes insane being alone with the boys. He's already called me five times. *Five.* And every time, in a state of emergency."

"You should have brought them."

"But what about *my* vacation?" She laughed and rubbed my shoulder.

She whistled low when she saw the row of beer bottles on their way to the recycling, along with two whiskey bottles. Michael Beck had helped substantially with those. Our meetings had been proceeding smoothly, more or less, going on three weeks. I had discovered that alcohol, in moderated amounts, helped me tolerate his presence, and so we had a drink or three nearly every time he came around. It was more than I liked to drink, but we would be done by December.

"That's not all my doing," I said.

"Who's the bad influence?"

"A journalist. He's writing a profile." I half-rolled my eyes before she could gush. "It's not a big thing. It's kind of a pain, really. I've got to give him your e-mail one of these days, by the way. He'll have a few questions. I told him to go easy."

"Oh, I hope he doesn't." Her eyes glittered with mischief. "I'll tell him all your secrets." She carried her tiny suitcase toward the basement. "You're still smoking," she called from the stairs. "I can smell it."

"Now and then," I answered abstractedly. I was texting Michael. It was Friday and I didn't want him showing up.

I kept the text straightforward: **I have company this weekend. I'll see you on Monday.** I frowned as I pocketed my phone. Having Michael around wasn't "kind of a pain," as I had led Rachel to believe. It was the only thing I looked forward to anymore.

17

MICHAEL

Coral Diana DeWitt was difficult to find. Cal had never mentioned his ex-wife's name, and neither had the other profiles I'd read. I doubled back and checked them. Most didn't reference the divorce at all. Two articles alluded to it, but only in passing.

I Googled Cal's full name and the words marriage, divorce, and wedding announcement in every possible permutation. I found nothing.

Was divorce a matter of public record? I Googled that, too, and discovered that the right lawyer could seal nearly any document.

I continued to comb the Internet (and add different words to my search) until, at last, I stumbled onto a DeWitt family reunion event page. It dated back to 2011 and listed Caleb David Bright, Coral Diana DeWitt-Bright, and Caleb Seth DeWitt-Bright Jr. as guests. Cal was thirty-one now, meaning he would have been twenty-six then. I scribbled a few more calculations on a notepad.

He had moved to Colorado four years ago, in 2012.

His son was five, so he'd had the child when he was twenty-six.

His three novels had been published between 2007 and 2012, the first when he was just twenty-two years old, an instant literary sensation.

I chewed on my pen cap and stared at the figures. What had happened in 2012, when he had stopped publishing, quite possibly divorced his wife, left his one-year-old son, and moved to the middle of nowhere, alone?

I wrote and underlined the question: <u>What happened in 2012?</u>

Having found his ex-wife's full name, I easily located a few former addresses and landline numbers. The most recent address placed her at a gated community in Charleston, South Carolina. I wrote down the number.

Guilt pricked at me as I tapped the digits into my phone. Cal had said that his ex "wouldn't comment" and that I didn't "want to deal with her." But what if she would comment, and what if I did want to deal with her? There had been no mistaking his meaning, though. He didn't want me talking to her.

But three weeks had passed since my first meeting with Cal and we weren't making any progress. Sure, he no longer slammed me into walls or snapped at me for falling, and yes, he had been very forthcoming about his rosy upbringing, but I was no closer to knowing him. If anything, he was holding me back—deliberately, effortlessly—from any real or nuanced understanding of his life. And it was infuriating.

I had promised him that I wouldn't publish anything private, and besides, he and his agent would give the profile their final approval (or disapproval). If I was going to write about Cal at all, though, I needed to see him completely.

Now I understood why the other profiles on Cal were superficial and trite. He had probably fed those journalists the same bullshit he was feeding me. Maybe they had tried to get below the surface and he hadn't let them, either. It hurt me, though. Looking back, I guess that was the truest sign of my inexperience. It hurt me that he didn't trust me. It hurt me that I couldn't be the exception to his rules.

So I called his ex-wife, and to hell with his feelings on the matter.

The phone rang again and again, until I was sure it would go to a machine, and then someone with a sleepy, lilting voice, and the barest trace of a southern accent answered. "Hello?" she said.

Something about the voice, and even the five or six rings before it answered, made me sit up straighter. I pictured that voice belonging to a southern belle in a milk bath. I pictured my phone call invading a warm, leisurely afternoon.

"Hello," I said. "May I please speak to Ms. Coral DeWitt?"

"This is she."

"Oh, hello. This is Michael Beck"—I hesitated—"with *The New Yorker*. I'm writing a profile on your . . . on Caleb Bright."

"I really have nothing to say about that." She sounded embarrassed.

"I was hoping you could give me some insight into his relationship with his son," I said, because asking this woman about her relationship with Cal seemed suddenly, incredibly off the table. Cal had been right; I shouldn't have imposed on his ex-wife like this, but curiosity pushed me forward. "Anything you could tell me would help."

She was silent for a while.

Then, carefully, she said, "He doesn't see his son."

I blinked. "No?" Cal had told me that he saw his son whenever he wanted.

"Well, we barely see one another. And I don't think you should be asking me about it." Her delicate voice cut me down completely. "Who did you say you are, again?"

Cal was going to murder me if he found out about this: This disclosure of information, even this call.

"I'm sorry," I stammered. "I'm very sorry. You're right. I'll let you go."

"I don't think you should call again."

"No, you're right. I apologize."

"Goodbye." She hung up.

18

CALEB

Rachel is easy company. She likes to do the same five things every time we're together: Go to church, ride horseback in the mountains, build campfires at night, cook, and play instruments and sing together.

As soon as she got settled in the guest room, she came upstairs carrying my violin case. "I've missed this so much," she said with a sigh.

I wasn't really in the mood for music, but I have never been able to say no to my little sister. And maybe it would cheer me up.

"You want the violin or the guitar?" I said.

"What I really want is for you to get a piano."

"It would only be for you. You know I'm awful."

"Well, aren't I worth it?" She batted her lashes. "And I don't think you're *awful*."

I smiled and shook my head. "I'll take the guitar, then." I wandered out to the annex, where I kept my painting supplies and two acoustic guitars. The guitars got very little attention—so did the paintings, lately—but I picked one up sometimes when a painting was proving frustrating.

I had to hunt for the black and red hymnbooks we liked to play from, and I was still rummaging around when I heard Michael's voice in the house.

19

MICHAEL

On Friday morning, I told Nicole how I had caught Cal in a lie. I desperately needed to talk to someone about it and there was no one else I trusted.

"So ask him about it," she said. She was in a rush, getting ready for work, and only half-listening to me.

"I'm not sure I should. He's going to be pissed."

"A real journalist would confront him."

"Nic, he might actually attack me."

"Because you called his ex? That's part of your job."

"No, it's not." I sighed. "This isn't like, the *National Enquirer*. It's *The New Yorker*. It's literary. It's—"

"If I don't get it, why are you asking for my opinion?" She smudged her mascara and swore. "You're blocking my light."

She made a fair point. I shuffled out of the bathroom and parked myself at the kitchen table. When she came in to make her coffee, I tried again.

"I just really, really need to make some progress on this profile. I can't crack it. I can't even get a first paragraph."

"I hope it ends up being worthwhile. It's stressing you out so much, and it's kind of killing your stream."

"It's not killing my stream." Nicole was fond of hyperbole. "And it's not stressing me out . . . much. I mean, it wouldn't stress me as much if he'd give me a little honesty. I actually want to be his friend, you know? But maybe he feels like I'm not good enough." I was mostly talking to myself, mumbling and stirring my Lucky Charms. "That's one of my theories. He was crazy successful at a young age; his parents are clearly loaded; he went to Harvard. He could just be a snob."

Nicole made a neutral noise.

"Except he doesn't give off that vibe," I persisted. "Not often, anyway. I think he could—he *could* be a snob if he wanted. I think he actually tries not to. God, you should have heard his ex, though. She was basically Daisy Buchanan. She—"

"Who?"

"From—never mind. It's hard to explain, but I could tell she was rich and cultured and it was like, she wanted to hang up on me, but she *made* herself say goodbye. Genteel, you know? It was intimidating. And he was married to that."

"You are full-on obsessed with this guy." Nicole glanced up from her phone. "Seriously, if you could hear yourself."

I frowned at her. "I kind of have to be. I'm writing about him."

"That doesn't mean you have to be his friend. I may not know everything about literary stuff"—oh, so she was pissed about that—"but I know you can't write objectively if you're biased. Pretty sure that's Journalism 101. Anyway, I'm late."

"I'll see you tonight," I said without looking at her. I was a little pissed, too. She was trying to make me feel crazy, like I was under Caleb Bright's spell, which was the opposite of what I needed to feel. I was, in fact, intentionally avoiding that line of thought, because it seemed so obvious and inevitable. Cal was older than I was, more successful, ridiculously educated, and part of a world of privilege I had only read about in books—and he seemed to be hurting, hiding something. Of course I was fixated on him. Show me the journalist who wouldn't be.

I drove out to Red Feather, my thoughts spinning.

Today, maybe, I would politely refuse the drinks that Cal would definitely offer. He always said he didn't like to drink alone, but alcohol wasn't helping me around him. It was making me easier for him to manipulate. It was also making him seem slightly alcoholic, which was one of my theories vis-à-vis his divorce.

He doesn't see his son . . .

The words ran continually through my mind.

If I fessed up to calling his ex, he would probably punch me in the face. If I tried to let it go, curiosity would eat me alive. Which was the lesser evil?

I parked, walked up the drive, and let myself into his house, as usual. That day, I paid extra attention to my steps. It seemed like a fall-on-my-face kind of day.

Maybe that's why I didn't see the woman (or her car in the driveway) until I practically ran into her.

She made a small, startled noise, and we both dropped back a step.

It was Cal's sister, standing in his family room, holding a violin. I recognized her instantly from the photo album. By some unnatural craft, she had become more attractive with age. The spray of freckles across her nose gave her an impish look and her heavy black hair was slightly disheveled, tumbling around her shoulders. She wore a cream-colored sweater, as if she had dressed to match Cal's luxurious decor, and the scent of lilacs hung around her.

The sight of her knocked me speechless.

She appeared equally stunned, her mouth open and her eyebrows raised.

No, she actually appeared more stunned—more stunned by the second. Her face paled and she pressed the violin to her chest. Then she laughed unsteadily and reached a hand toward me. "Who are you?" she said.

By this time, my stomach had begun to churn. I was not supposed to be here. Cal would never have sprung this on me. I touched my pocket and my stomach dropped. I had left my phone at home—no surprise, considering my state of mind that morning.

"I'm so sorry," I said, backing toward the door. "I think I'm not supposed to be here. I'm, uh, interviewing Cal—Caleb."

She followed me, looking one part mesmerized, one part afraid. Before I could backpedal out the door, she clutched my coat sleeve. "You *must* be related to Jamie Foust," she said. Her smile was heartbreakingly hopeful.

"No, I . . ." I shook my head. *Jamie Foust*. The name meant nothing to me.

At that moment, Cal materialized, moving swiftly toward the door. His expression was murderous. His sister couldn't see it— she was still searching my face, clinging to my coat—but I could, and I wanted to run.

"Rachel," he murmured. "I'm sorry. This is the journalist. I wasn't expecting him." His eyes flickered to me. "I texted you."

"I'm so sorry. My phone, I left my phone—"

"I don't mind." Rachel laughed musically. Her composure had returned. She was all that stood between her potentially homicidal brother and me, and now I wanted to cling to her. "Cal, be nice. I really don't mind."

"I do. Go look for the red and black hymnals, please. They should be in the annex." He held a guitar case, which might soon double as a weapon. He set it on the floor. His sister flashed an apologetic smile at me.

"Well, it was nice to meet you, Mr. Journalist." As she passed Cal, she squeezed his shoulder and whispered harshly, "Be nice."

Then she was gone. I smiled feebly as Cal descended. For one horrible moment, I wondered if his ex-wife had contacted him. He seized my arm in a crushing grip and marched me out of his house. I'd never felt so young in the twenty-fifth year of my life.

"I'm sorry," I stammered, stumbling along. "I really am sorry. My phone—"

"I *heard* you," he snarled. He escorted me all the way to my car. To his credit, he didn't open the door and shove me behind the wheel. He simply released me and stepped back, visibly collecting himself. "My sister . . ."

"Yes." I stared at my feet. I had interrupted a family get-together. I had frightened his sister, somehow. I had also heard a name that might mean something in the puzzle of Cal: *Jamie Foust*. "I . . . Cal, I'm sorry. She's visiting. And you texted, so I wouldn't interrupt. I swear, I really did forget my phone. I would never—"

He raised a hand, sensing, maybe, that I was about to turn out my pockets to prove I hadn't received his text and decided to ambush them anyway. "I believe you."

"Okay. I'll go."

"Yes, I think you'd better."

I was fumbling with the car door when he touched my shoulder. I could count on one hand the number of times he had touched me, all of them in anger, so it shocked me. I spun around. He was wearing the strangest smile, which fell just short of inviting.

"Listen," he said. "Did she say anything to you?"

It was an odd question, a paranoid question. "She . . . well, she asked who I was." That wasn't the whole truth, but it also wasn't a lie.

"Ah. You probably surprised her."

"Yeah. I really am sorry."

"She probably surprised you, too." He wasn't trying to make conversation; he was peering at me, trying to gauge my sincerity. I ducked into the car.

"She did, yeah." I laughed weakly. "You're both a little . . . intimidating."

"Oh, I hope so." He nodded and closed my door.

20

CALEB

My expression darkened as soon as Michael pulled out of the drive. He was lying to me, definitely—not about missing my text, but about what my sister had said.

I walked back up to the house.

Rachel was tuning the violin.

"So that was the bad influence," she said.

I smirked and sat beside her. She couldn't possibly guess how right she was.

"Yeah. I'm sorry he showed up." I unlatched the guitar case. I felt even less like music now, and especially hymns, but my family's musicality had its roots in worship music. Our father and mother played half a dozen instruments and sang harmony, and so did we. Music had been a part of every church service in my youth. Even now, the little Bible chapel I attended occasionally prevailed upon me to play an instrument or sing. I did it, too, because it made the people so happy.

"I wish you hadn't sent him away," she said. "You didn't need to do that."

"This is our time. I'm not having some journalist here, prying into our lives."

"He seemed sweet."

My teeth clenched reflexively. "If, by sweet, you mean naïve and impressionable, I guess you're right."

"You know . . ." She frowned and lowered the violin. I knew what was coming. Her long fingers played over the bridge and I sat, tense, braced. "It was so strange, seeing him. He looks almost exactly like Jamie Foust." She looked to me for confirmation.

"He does." I nodded. There was no denying it. "I've had the same thought."

"That must be hard." She squeezed my hand.

"Well, it's been a while."

"Still, that poor boy. You always kind of wonder what goes on in people's lives, right? His family was so faithful, so solid."

I felt like someone was dragging razors over my insides. But I'd had years of practice saying the right things in the right voices. I shrugged and rested the guitar across my lap. "I think he got away from his faith in college. That school in Boulder is very liberal. Lots of partying and that kind of stuff."

"Well, that'll do it. Drugs just take people down."

"Yeah. So, who knows where his life went after that? I mean, we lost touch. He stopped going to camp, too." That was the truth, as far as Rachel was concerned. She had never known about the apartment in Virginia and she never would.

"What a sad thing." She sighed and shook her head. "But that journalist, how crazy. It was like seeing a ghost. Cal, I think I freaked him out. I got such a shock, I even asked if he was related to Jamie."

I stiffened. "Oh, did you?"

"Yes! The poor kid."

Michael was only four years younger than Rachel, but I understood completely why she called him a kid. Compared to us, to me, he seemed so childish. I remembered Jamie having that same quality—an irrepressible, wide-eyed wonder.

"I wouldn't worry about it," I said. "He was probably too busy staring at you to notice anything else."

She brightened and gave me a nudge. "Flatterer." She snickered. "He *was* staring, though, like a deer in headlights."

My fingers moved over the guitar with a gentleness that surprised me. I strummed an A minor. In my mind, I was driving my fists into granite.

"But we had so much fun at Camp Apache, didn't we?" she said. "I can't wait until the boys are old enough to go." She must have sensed that I was sad. She was trying to cheer me up.

Fortunately, I was a much better actor than Michael. I smiled fondly and nodded.

"So much fun," I said. "The best memories."

21

MICHAEL

Jamie Foust could have been my twin brother, we looked so alike, and Jamie Foust was dead. I wasted no time finding his obituary online.

Jamie Adam Foust, 27, passed away March 3, 2012. Survived by his father and mother, numerous aunts, uncles, and cousins. Preceded in death by his grandparents. Jamie was born January 15, 1985, in Dallas, Texas. He was a talented poet and artist. Graduate of University of Colorado Boulder. There will be no viewing. Memorials may be sent to . . .

I printed the page.

The small, grainy picture accompanying the obituary showed a clean-shaven young man with my pale brown hair and eyes, my uncertain smile, and my prominent cheekbones. No wonder I had alarmed Cal's sister. And, if Cal had known Jamie, maybe my resemblance explained his initial reaction, too.

I turned in my office chair slowly. A new constellation of questions was forming around me. Who was Jamie Foust to Cal, if anyone? How had Jamie died? And was it a coincidence that he had died in 2012, the year Cal's golden life unraveled?

"It has to mean something," I muttered to Furio, who was watching me swivel in my chair. "Otherwise, why did he ask me what his sister said? He had to be worried I'd find out about this." I waved the printed page.

Now that I had found out about Jamie Foust, though, I was in another deadlock. Asking Cal about Jamie meant confessing my lie (and my shameless research), just like asking about his nonexistent visitation rights meant admitting I had called his ex-wife.

(That quote about weaving tangled webs is appropriate here.)

I scoured the Internet for any connection between Caleb Bright and Jamie Foust, but there was nothing. I stared at Jamie Foust's photo for a long time, as if he might come alive and tell me everything, and then, when that got too unsettling, I crumpled the page and dropped it in the trash.

22

CALEB

I FORTIFIED MYSELF WITH A drink before Michael arrived on Monday. By now, he must have considered me borderline alcoholic, and maybe I was getting there. I took no pleasure in the drinking, though, and I couldn't wait to stop. But it helped, like foul-tasting medicine. My whiskey-soaked brain functioned on one cylinder, and that was a good thing. Being in a state of mental acuity around him was simply too painful, and too . . .

I gazed at my reflection as I brushed my teeth.

I wouldn't admit it to myself, even in the vault of my mind. I hoped that effort meant something to God when he looked at my heart.

Michael let himself in as I was making my coffee, per usual. Our meetings had fallen into a comfortable rhythm. (They had been comfortable previously, at least.)

"Good morning," he said.

To be on the safe side, I was assuming the worst: That Michael had looked up Jamie Foust, that he knew Jamie was dead, knew about their uncanny resemblance, and knew that I hadn't wanted my sister (or anyone) to mention it.

In short, I was safely assuming that Michael knew I was hiding something. Whether he had the guts to ask me anything remained to be seen.

"Hello," I said.

I thought I detected a new air of anxiety about him—a thin film of unease as he settled on the couch with his laptop.

"Did you have a nice time with your sister?"

"Very, thank you." I leaned against the counter and sipped my coffee, watching the back of his head. "She has a habit of dropping by unannounced. Always has. I'm sorry I couldn't give you more notice."

"It's not your fault. I'm the one who's sorry."

"*Ad absurdum*. I wish I were keeping a running tally of your apologies."

"S—" He stopped himself short of another compulsive apology. "I didn't know you played an instrument."

I had left my violin on the coffee table, calculatedly, to spur conversation about anything but Jamie. Poor Michael always took the bait.

"Yes, a few. That, the guitar, some of the woodwinds, and a little piano, but very poorly. Rachel is the real pianist. Our mother, too."

"I'd love to hear you play."

"Sure, some time."

"You two were going to play together?" He bent over his laptop, typing.

"We were, yeah. We did. She likes us to play hymns and harmonize."

His head came up. "You sing?"

"Yes." I roamed into the family room, set down my coffee, and lifted the violin. I nestled it under my chin and drew the bow across a string. One perfect, liquid note sang from the wooden body. I was aware of Michael staring. From time to time,

I let him. "Music was a big part of our worship services, growing up. Music and singing."

"So your parents made you learn?"

"We wanted to learn. It gave us joy. Gives us joy." I set down the violin and moved out of his field of vision.

"Your sister—"

"Rachel."

"Rachel." He cleared his throat. "She seemed nice."

"Did she?" I blew a curl of steam off my coffee. "How so?"

He became instantly flustered, gesturing and shaking his head. "Well, I mean, sweet. No, um . . . friendly. Charming."

"Sweet?" I suppressed laughter. This was easy, and too fun. "Charming? What exactly are you trying to say, Michael?"

He caught my mocking tone and fell silent.

"Sorry." I chuckled. "She's a card. Really, she's adorable, isn't she?" I moved back around the couch so I could watch his expression. His neck was faintly flushed.

"She's very nice."

"Don't you think she's pretty?" I grinned into my mug.

"Well, sure." He glared at his laptop, heat creeping into his face. "You both . . . definitely got lucky with the gene pool."

"Hm." I moved away again. "How's your girlfriend?"

The question caught him off guard, probably because we rarely discussed his life.

"She's fine, thanks. Normal."

"Yeah?"

"Yeah."

Michael tended to fill silences with chatter, as if he could singlehandedly build our camaraderie, so I let him stew for a moment—and, sure enough, he started up again.

"We don't see much of each other, lately. Ships passing in the night, kind of thing." He explained his new streaming schedule, of which I was aware. Unbeknownst to Michael, I checked his Twitter, blog, and stream regularly. "So, when I'm not here, I'm usually in the basement streaming. Basement office, that is."

I made an understanding noise.

He continued.

"Or I'm writing blog posts, or smashing my face against this profile." He laughed uneasily. "She gets home from work and sometimes she'll bring down Subway or Chik-fil-A. That might be all we see of each other in a given day. That and the morning. She goes to bed pretty early, so she's usually asleep when I finish streaming or writing."

"Romantic," I said.

"Yeah, really. We used to meet for lunch, but that kind of fell by the wayside."

"I hope all this isn't . . ." I gestured vaguely to my home.

He caught my meaning and turned to look at me emphatically. "No, this is great. Journalism is what I want to do. She and I are fine. Or, I mean, these meetings aren't . . ."

"Good. I wouldn't want to strain things."

I stepped out to smoke and, for the first time, Michael plucked up the courage to follow. I glanced at him warily. I used my periodic smoke breaks to get away from him. It made our otherwise constant closeness tolerable.

"Do you mind?" he said.

"Of course not," I lied.

"I love it out here. The view, the cold."

I pictured him in his "basement office" and I wanted to say he could visit any time.

I stood at the railing and he stood at my side. When I lit my cigarette, I moved away. "Second-hand smoke," I explained.

"That's okay. I don't care."

"I do. It's not good for you."

"But it's okay for you?"

I gave him a sharp look. "Yes," I said. "That's right."

23

CALEB

That afternoon, I showed Michael my paintings. The annex smelled of linseed oil and paint, which I loved, but I opened the broad eastern and western windows to air it out. I didn't need him fainting on me.

He was respectful verging on timid, as always. He wouldn't so much as move a finished canvas to view the one behind it.

"Go ahead," I said when I saw him hovering over my sketchbooks. I had already removed everything related to Jamie.

He leafed through the sketches. He drifted from one canvas to another like a bumblebee. He passed the tips of his fingers near my brushes, paint tubes, and palettes, and then he circled the room again, repeating the process.

"You're really good," he finally said. He sounded sad.

I didn't need Michael Beck's stamp of approval on my artwork, but I wanted it. I had been waiting, anticipating his reaction, and the three words let me down.

"What's the matter?" I said. "Don't like abstracts? Some of these are landscapes. I did them out on the ridge." I moved toward a pile of canvases.

"No, they're all really good," he repeated. "I like modern stuff."

"Then what is it?"

"I'm only good at computer games." He turned toward his laptop, away from me.

"That's not true. I've read your blog. You're a great writer."

"You're better," he replied immediately.

I wanted to laugh. Where was this juvenile self-pity coming from? "Michael"—I tried to sound reasonable—"don't compare us." I knew the words were a mistake the moment they left my mouth.

He tucked his laptop under his arm and headed for the family room. "Yeah, exactly. Why would I ever do that?"

"That came out wrong." I followed him.

"No, it came out right. I mean, we aren't from the same world."

"Is this about the profile? Are you having trouble with it?"

"Of course I'm having trouble with it." He laughed, exasperated. "You won't tell me anything about your ex, your son, whatever the hell happened . . ."

I knew he wanted to add Jamie Foust to that list. I could practically hear it on the tip of his tongue. I took a breath and looked away.

"What is it?" he said. "Please."

"Just phone it in," I said quietly. It was my plea back to him, but he appeared horrified at the suggestion.

"Are you kidding me?"

I headed for the kitchen and a drink. I couldn't possibly have looked like I was kidding. I felt blanched and off balance, and dangerously close to blurting out the truth. But when I turned back to face him, he was gone.

2 4

MICHAEL

I DROVE BACK TO BOULDER, wavering between anger and pity. *Just phone it in.* Cal had actually begged me to half-ass the profile. Whatever he didn't want me to know, it was also the source of his pain, and he was unwilling or unable to talk about it.

Did he have such a low opinion of me, though, that he thought I would compromise my work ethic? I never half-assed anything, not even comedic blog posts, and I definitely would not *phone in* an article for *The New Yorker*. The suggestion was ridiculous and inappropriate.

Still, I had driven him to suggest it. I had mentioned his ex, his son, and "whatever the hell happened," i.e. Jamie Foust, and Cal had gone sheet-white and lunged at the nearest alcoholic beverage. I had no right to terrorize him like that—not in the name of journalism, not in the name of anything.

So I went back and forth, back and forth from frustration to sympathy, and I didn't stream on Tuesday, and I didn't go to Red Feather on Wednesday. I sent him a text, claiming I was "feeling unwell." It was sort of true, like most of what he told me.

Get better, he texted back, **it's quiet without your questions**.

I couldn't tell if he was mocking me or missing my company.

The problem was, going to Red Feather again and again was becoming the definition of insanity. We had toured his property, visited the horse he boarded down the road, gone to his church (twice) and the farmers' market, marathoned most of *The Sopranos* and *Game of Thrones*, and endured countless conversations that resembled fencing matches. And the profile wasn't getting written. I still had no idea what had driven him to stop publishing—his explanations were flimsy, at best—and no real sense of his interior life.

So, on Thursday, when Nicole suggested we have a mini-party on Friday, an idea popped into my head like a revelation.

"Definitely," I told her, with the express intention of inviting Cal.

Cal and I were always at his house, on his terms.

Maybe I just needed to get him out of the mountains.

25

CALEB

"A PARTY?" I FROWNED AT Michael. I was glad to see him—truly, I was—but desperation seemed to be affecting his head.

"It's more of a get-together, really. Just some friends, drinks. You know."

I didn't know. "Boulder is kind of a long drive," I hedged.

"Oh, I'll drive. I was thinking you could crash on the couch."

I forced my expression to remain neutral. I had not "crashed" on anyone's "couch" in over five years. "Your couch?"

"Yeah. It's . . . about this size." He patted my couch. "So, it's long."

"And this is tonight?"

"Yeah. It's informal. No pressure."

He looked eager in a way that I had never seen him, so I knew what this idea was: Michael's last-ditch effort to form a meaningful connection with me.

No pressure, indeed.

I weighed my options quickly: Decline the invitation and risk alienating him completely, or say yes and spend one miserable evening among drunken pseudo-adults.

Since my argument with Michael on Monday, I was increasingly aware that I needed to give him something, anything, to make him feel trustworthy. He wasn't a moron. He knew I was feeding him half-truths and lines, but he hadn't yet resorted to guerilla tactics (contacting my family behind my back, bringing up Jamie Foust). I almost couldn't believe he hadn't mentioned Jamie yet, but I was quietly grateful.

Michael was being decent.

Meanwhile, I was being irrational, advising him to phone in an article that had to be quite a big deal for his career.

It wouldn't kill me to tell him a few things about Coral, or to go to his party.

"Well," I said, "I haven't been to Boulder in a while," and his face lit up.

2 6

CALEB

I PACKED AN OVERNIGHT BAG and climbed into Michael's Jeep with a mounting sense of dread. It would have been too freakish, really, to try to sit in back, or even to pregame on the road. Both thoughts crossed my mind, though.

"I hope you won't be offended if I doze off," I said preemptively. "Long drives tend to put me to sleep."

Sleep (or feigned sleep) was the obvious solution: Eyes closed, ignoring his suffocating proximity.

"No, not at all. Do you like music? I mean, not if you're sleeping. Well, I know you like music. I won't play anything now. If you want to sleep now. Anything works."

I smirked and gazed out my window.

Michael felt just as agitated as I did, clearly, but whereas I clamped down on my anxiety with rigid control, he tended to jitter right off the handle. It was amusing.

"Whatever you want," I said, closing my eyes.

"Are you going to sleep? I mean, what do you want? Should we stop for food?"

"Michael." I sighed through my teeth. "Drive."

The Jeep handled horribly on the dirt roads surrounding my house. Or, I should say, it handled like a Jeep, vibrating and jolting as if every pebble were a boulder. I couldn't even pretend to be asleep, so I opened my eyes and glared at the scenery.

"I need to adjust the shocks on this thing!" Michael hollered over the incessant rattling. "It'll be smoother on the pavement! Sorry! I love dirt roads, though!"

I lifted a hand in a tolerant gesture.

"How does the Audi do on these roads?"

I had no desire to raise my voice, so I made another gesture. *It does fine.*

"And you've got the Cadillac CTS, right?"

Another gesture. *Yes.*

"Great cars!"

Thumbs up.

"They do okay with the snow?"

I nodded.

"I guess you get a ton of snow out here!"

Affirmative motion.

He finally relaxed enough to stop shouting out conversation, but the peace was short-lived. When we reached a paved road and relative silence filled the car, he started up again. "That's much better, right? Dang, this car is so noisy. I'm sorry."

"It's fine, really."

"What kind of music do you like?"

"All kinds."

"Older stuff? Newer stuff?"

"A bit of everything."

"I just bought this sick cover of 'Dust in the Wind.' It's by Digital Daggers. I heard it on a *WoW: Legion* trailer." He plugged in his phone and played the song. "I have a ton of the music from *Game of Thrones*, too. You'd probably like that. It's mostly instrumental. Really cool stuff."

He would have talked and played music for the next two hours if I hadn't intervened. "Listen," I said, "do you mind if I smoke?"

"Oh, not at all. Go for it."

I turned off the music and lowered my window, lit a cigarette, and closed my eyes. "My ex-wife," I said. "She's from one of the first families in South Carolina. Society, kind of. Our families knew each other through mission work, church stuff. We were basically pushed together for her deb ball. Those are big in the south. Anyway, I was going to Harvard at the time, and her mother thought I'd be a good escort."

A thick silence had descended in the Jeep.

I knew, if I opened my eyes and looked over, that I would find Michael poised, unblinking, petrified of breaking whatever spell had loosened my tongue.

"So, we took a trip down for that. I remember . . . the weather. The atmosphere. It was all very . . . romantic, I guess, like something out of *The Great Gatsby*. And Coral, she refused to wear white like all the other debs. She changed at the last minute. I thought her mother was going to have an aneurysm." I chuckled and took a drag. I remembered it with perfect clarity: Coral and I making our entrance, Coral wearing a peach satin gown that clung to every curve, and her mother's face getting redder and redder.

And everyone staring.

And my pride at having that slightly insane, bold girl on my arm.

"She was truly the belle of the ball," I said.

I described the gown to Michael and how, because it was expected and logical, Coral and I had started dating long distance. I told him how we used to meet when we could, how beautiful and fiery she was, and how, in a moment of mutual competition, and in spite of our straitlaced upbringings, we'd had sex and she had gotten pregnant.

"It was a very big deal, in families like ours. It was a horrible shock for everyone. We got married right away."

I left it there, and Michael was silent for the rest of the drive.

27

MICHAEL

Cal was an object of fascination at the mini-party, which rapidly morphed into less of a *mini-party* and more of a *I hope I've built up enough goodwill with the neighbors that they don't call the cops* kind of thing. That was Nicole's fault. I had ordered her to tell no one about Caleb Bright's invitation, and she had selectively not heard the order and told a dozen of her work friends about the "big deal author" coming to our house.

And suddenly the street was lined with cars and we had thirty people, at least, milling around our cramped home and postage stamp of a yard. Furio was terrified. He kept emerging from under the bed, whining, running, searching for us, and hiding again.

I wouldn't have blamed Cal if he had gotten under the bed himself. Instead, he bore the attention with gentlemanly grace. I brought him drinks and tried my best to steer him away from people, but no matter where we went, there was someone, someone slightly uninhibited by alcohol, asking if he was The Author.

It didn't help that he stood out like a sore thumb. The expensive denim, the leather jacket, the height, the good looks, the ponytail only he could pull off—there was no hiding him. "I'm so sorry," I kept mumbling.

"Michael, it's fine," he kept replying.

But it was not fine. He had only agreed to attend the party out of guilt—the same reason, no doubt, that he'd held forth about his ex-wife in the car. My tantrum on Monday and my absence on Wednesday had actually worried him, and so he was trying to appease me.

I felt like scum.

The worst part of the evening began when someone broke a glass in the kitchen and Nicole asked me to clean it up. I had to abandon Cal for a full fifteen minutes. When I returned to the packed living room, I saw that a girl—a friend of Nicole—was literally dancing on Cal. He wasn't dancing; he was holding his beer and leaning against the wall. But she was going crazy all over him, showing off her moves, grinding on him in ways that had to be destroying his will to live.

I knew how he hated to be touched. I wanted to shove her away, on his behalf.

I pushed through the crowd, watching Cal with drowning eyes.

"There you are!" I stammered when I reached him. "I was looking for you."

The girl, I thought her name was Kristin, had enough sense and sobriety to stop dancing when I appeared. She laid a hand on Cal's arm, though, like a claim.

"Hey, Mike," she said. "Great party."

Cal smiled evenly at me. "Did you get the kitchen under control?" He seemed relaxed, bored even. Maybe it was the calm before the storm.

"Yeah. Some of the glass went under the fridge, so."

"What a pain." He was on his fifth or sixth beer, which meant nothing, really. I had seen him put away half a bottle of whiskey and walk a straight line to the bathroom.

"Did someone break a glass?" maybe-Kristin said too loudly. "Freaking drunks. Seriously, there's some people who need to be cut off!"

"I agree," I said, staring at her.

Cal grinned faintly. I couldn't get a read on him. Maybe he had taken a powerful antipsychotic, or maybe he was actually enjoying himself.

"Did you want to see my stream setup now?" I ventured. "Remember I wanted to show you, in the office?"

"Sure, if you like."

"No, you're not stealing him yet!" Maybe-Kristin sulked. "We were just talking about his books."

Yes, I had definitely seen her *talking* about his *books* with her butt on his crotch.

"Well"—I looked between them—"whenever, I mean . . ."

"Later, then," Cal murmured. "I'd love to see it, Michael."

I had thrown him a life preserver and he had tossed it back in my face, which could only mean that he was enjoying maybe-Kristin's butt on his crotch. Which seemed impossible. I gave him one more careful look before wandering away.

Could it be that, all this time, Cal had only needed to get laid? Would he go home with maybe-Kristin? Or was he trying to prove, to the nth degree, that he was having a good time at my party? That last thought was intolerable.

I got myself a new beer, chugged it, got another, and found Nicole.

Maybe Cal, even in my own home, didn't want to be around me. Maybe I was somehow more annoying than maybe-Kristin.

"Kristin is adorable with Cal," Nicole said.

So she was definitely-Kristin.

"Yeah, I guess. I hope she isn't bugging him."

"Are you kidding? Look at them."

I glanced over. Kristin had removed Cal's hair tie and was finger-combing the long pieces. He was laughing, albeit inattentively.

"How much has she had to drink?"

"Mike, she's *fine*." Nicole frowned at me.

"Okay, okay. I'm just looking out for my friend."

"I don't think he needs any help. Also, why didn't you tell me he's so . . ." She blinked a few times. "I don't know. He's crazy fit."

Fit. My own girlfriend wanted to say Cal was hot, but instead she said *fit*. Someday, with a bunch of aliases, I would write a scathing blog post about tonight. No one would be spared, except for Cal. Cal would be suffering quietly on his cross while Kristin played with his hair and danced against his crotch. Saint Caleb. Caleb the martyr.

I drank too much and mingled. I tried to keep an eye on Cal, in case he should need extraction, but I lost track of him again around midnight. The party had thinned by then. I turned down and slowed down the music—Radiohead, Elliott Smith, and Bon Iver—and a few people migrated outside to smoke.

"Did Kristin go home?" I asked Nicole. I was hoping, praying, that Cal hadn't gone home with her. I knew that I had passive-aggressively pushed him into talking about his ex-wife and attending my stupid party, and I wouldn't be able to forgive myself if I had also indirectly driven him into a one-night stand.

"Um, I don't think so?" Nicole swayed and held my shoulder for support. "Maybe she went outside? I'm not sure."

I pulled on my coat and went out to the deck. The cold air sobered me a little.

A cluster of people sat and sprawled in the grass around our fire pit. The smell of weed mingled with the smell of campfire and the smell of autumn. I recognized Cal's figure in the flickering light. Kristin hit a pipe and exhaled the smoke into his mouth, which I thought people only did in movies. Then he took a hit and passed it.

I gripped the deck railing so tightly that my hands went numb.

Kristin was halfway draped over Cal. She whispered in his ear and started to kiss his neck. His dark eyes suddenly flickered to mine and he smiled.

My face went from cold to hot in a second.

I lifted my hand, waved lamely, as if I had just seen him. As if I hadn't been watching. His smile broadened slowly. He seemed so detached from what Kristin was doing. His hands were planted in the grass, arms braced, and he leaned back as if he were sitting there alone, enjoying the night.

I couldn't look away.

He held my gaze while Kristin's mouth moved over his throat.

My pulse beat louder and louder in my ears.

He wasn't smiling anymore, and there was something new and indecipherable in his gaze. When he finally dismissed Kristin, it was like she had never existed. He stood and she slipped off his lap and he just walked away.

Dick move, I thought. So why did I want to cheer?

He came directly to me. "I'm tired," he said.

"Lemme . . . yeah. Gimme five seconds." I kicked everyone out of my house and yard, including Kristin, and picked up around the couch as well as I could. Cal tried to help, stacking a few cups. "Please, don't." I was slurring.

He shrugged and took his bag to the bathroom.

I knew it would be a mistake to try to apologize further or engage him at all, but I wanted to make sure he got settled. A good night's sleep was the least I could offer him.

I put two pillows and a sheet and blanket on the couch. I turned off the lamp and left on the kitchen light, which cast a dim glow down the hall.

I carried as many dishes and as much trash out of the room as I could, and then, on my third trip back, I found him stretched belly down on the couch, the blanket draped around his waist, arms folded on the pillow. His head was turned away. I couldn't tell if he was asleep or just very still.

His bare back seemed impossibly long. His hair was a liquid black spill.

He propped himself up on his forearms and gazed at me.

"Go to bed, Michael," he said after a while, and I fled.

When I climbed under the covers beside Nicole, I pressed myself ardently, impatiently against her. She mumbled something and rolled away. I slid a hand between her legs and she said, "Babe, I'm not in the mood," in such a way that I knew she was shutting me down in her sleep.

28

MICHAEL

THE NEXT MORNING, CAL WOKE and dressed before I did, and I found him drinking coffee on the deck. He looked incredibly out of place, like an eagle in a canary cage.

"Did you find everything?" I said.

"Nicole helped." He indicated the coffee.

"Cool. She left for yoga?"

He nodded and continued gazing across the yard. The "view" was laughable: One tree and a fence. Furio lay in a splash of sunshine, chewing on a stick.

"Not quite Red Feather Lakes, huh?" I tucked my hands in my pockets.

"It's very nice," he said. "Your home is also lovely. I appreciate the hospitality."

I wanted to tell him to cut the crap, but, with him, it was hard to tell where the crap ended and good breeding began. He probably did appreciate the hospitality, and he probably could find something nice to say about my house and yard.

"Is there anything you want to get while you're in Boulder?" I had no illusions about Cal wanting to stick around today, but it couldn't hurt to offer. He surprised me by considering for a while.

"A haircut, I think," he said.

I did a double take. "Oh. Great. There's a barber—"

"I'd rather go to a salon, if that's possible." He laughed. "I prefer to have a woman cut my hair when it's long. They know what they're doing."

"That makes sense." I fumbled with my phone. "Give me . . . one second. One minute." I darted inside.

I was pretty sure I had put Cal through hell last night and I was determined to make it up him. I texted Nicole (**what are the best salons in/around Boulder?**), made half a dozen calls, and got Cal an appointment at a high-end salon within the hour. When they asked for a credit card number for their cancellation policy, I paid for the cut up front. I even threw in an extra ten-minute scalp massage.

Never in my wildest dreams had I imagined this scenario, but I was glad for the chance to redeem Cal's experience in Boulder.

On the drive over, I awkwardly attempted conversation. "So, going short?"

"Oh, I don't know about that." He was imperturbable, staring out his window with eyes nearly closed. "I don't think so. Not very."

"Cool." I nodded. "The long hair works." I wondered if that was weird to say. "It works for you." Yes, it was definitely weird. "It works for the ladies." I made myself stop speaking then, because he was shaking with silent laughter.

The salon smelled like extreme hair product. I sneezed twice, rapidly, as soon as we stepped inside. The stylists were all petite and perfectly groomed and they offered Cal and me an impressive range of beverages, including wine and beer.

"Nothing for me, thanks." I sat on a couch in the waiting area.

"I'm fine." He waved them away. One pretty brunette stylist hovered. She looked like she couldn't wait to get her hands on Cal, which may have explained his *I'd rather go to a salon* specification. Maybe I would start going to salons, too. Cal was frowning down at me. "If you have errands to run . . ."

"No, I'll be okay. Go on." I smiled and looked busy on my laptop. I wasn't going anywhere until I was sure he had gotten exactly what he wanted that morning.

The stylist led Cal away, steering him with a hand on his back, and he sat at a station I could see. She ran her fingers through his hair, talking to him in the mirror and occasionally resting her hand on his shoulder or arm. Then they went off to shampoo. I heard her voice rising and falling, the words incomprehensible, the tone unmistakable. For a hundred and twenty dollars plus tip, I hoped he was having fun.

They emerged fifteen minutes later. She had her hand on his back again, low. When he sat, she brushed her breasts all too obviously over his arm. And it continued like that as she snipped away at his hair—the touching, the laughing and flirting—and Cal appeared tranquil, even pleasant. And I couldn't stop watching.

I was mesmerized, but I was also repelled.

Thick, wet pieces of hair fell like black feathers.

She rubbed his neck, said something about his hairline, and it hit me like a one-two punch. I sagged over my laptop.

One: The stylist's touch, like Kristin's touch last night, didn't bother Cal because it didn't mean a damn thing to him.

And two: I was jealous. I was jealous of those women, touching him so freely.

29

CALEB

Something was wrong with Michael. I had left him looking like his usual self, eager and anxious, near the front of the salon. By the time my cut was finished, though, he looked much as I must have the day he fell at my doorstep: Pale, shaken, and guarded.

"Is it that bad?" I asked casually as we walked out of the salon. I meant my hair, which was shorter by three inches and subtly layered. It hung in jagged, gleaming pieces around my jaw and against the back of my neck. I knew it looked damn good, so I couldn't fathom Michael's shock.

"Huh?" He barely glanced at me.

"Never mind." I frowned. "Hey, thank you for that. You shouldn't have."

He answered with a vague gesture. Oh, how the tables had turned.

"Is everything okay?" I said.

"What? Yeah. What's next?"

"Lunch, I suppose." I hadn't been planning to spend a single unnecessary second in Boulder, but Michael's mood needed unraveling.

"Sure. Where to?"

"You choose." I climbed into the Jeep.

He drove us to a Whole Foods Market, which I knew he had done for my sake. Given food choices, Michael tended toward the fast and the processed.

We both ordered chicken noodle soup and fruit and we ate at a table in the small dining area.

"So, what have I done to deserve this luxurious treatment?" I said.

He hunched over his meal, addressing the soup. "I'm just trying to show you a good—" He spluttered, choking on the words. "I mean, I feel bad. About the party."

"Why's that? I had a fine time."

He gave me a sudden and very clear-eyed look, as if he saw right through me. "Did you really?"

I glared at him. "Sure I did." Usually, with a glare, I could make him back down. Not today. His pale brown eyes were hard and steady.

"I thought Kristin might have had too much to drink."

"Was that her name?" I smirked.

"Yeah. She was all over you. I thought you might go home with her."

The idea turned my stomach. Still, I made myself chuckle and swallow a spoonful of soup. "Maybe I should have."

"I wonder how that would have gone." His tone was almost, almost sarcastic, and every instinct in my body told me to keep playing along. Or panic.

I went through the motions of finishing my soup while I sorted out what a normal response might be. I didn't taste the rest of the soup or hear anything around me.

"I'm ready to go," I said, and I headed out of the store blindly.

On the drive back to Red Feather, Michael tried a different tack.

"I'm sorry if that was rude, about Kristin." He sounded sincere. "I didn't mean that. There's nothing wrong—I mean—it's okay if you didn't have fun."

"I had fun," I said icily.

"Cal—"

"What? What's the matter with you?" I was terrified of his answer.

"Can I hang out today?"

"It's Saturday."

"Well, for our weekend day, since I'm driving all the way out."

"Fine," I said. "I honestly don't care."

30

MICHAEL

As soon as we got back, Cal said he wanted to run, and he stormed up to the loft and then out in his jogging clothes. I was not even remotely invited. I sat on his couch, in his achingly quiet home, while everything fell into place.

Jamie Foust.

Cal's short-lived marriage.

The way he flinched from me, couldn't stand to be near me.

The time he'd slammed me against the house for touching him.

His look of horror when I groaned over a delicious piece of pear, or when I peeled off a few layers to jog with him.

His offer, once, to get me a taxi and a hotel room. No sleeping here, of course.

And last night, the only moment he had actually lost control—not when Kristin was licking her way up his neck, but when I had come out to watch. Me. Little old me.

Thunder reverberated through the house and I jumped. I had been so involved in my thoughts that I hadn't noticed the gathering storm. It was afternoon, but the sky was evening black. Rain began to drive against the deck and windows. I moved to watch it sheeting over the lake. Wind roared out of the aspen and pines and they swayed like field grass.

Cal yanked open the deck door. I staggered back so sharply that I almost fell. His clothes were sodden, leaving puddles across the kitchen. I couldn't think of one thing to say. I couldn't believe I hadn't seen it sooner.

He kicked off his shoes and bolted upstairs to shower.

An hour passed before he came back down. The storm was still beating against the house and darkening the day unnaturally. He veered into the annex. I followed, wide eyed. The light was off and he was seated in one of two large wicker chairs, his easels moved aside. The walls were mostly windows and so, in that room, the electrical storm looked like a light show, pulsing white in the blue and purple clouds.

I pushed the other chair flush with his and sat. I could only hear my heart, then the thunder, then my heart. Without looking, I reached for his hand and pulled it over, onto my thigh. And then, so he couldn't mistake my intentions, I moved his hand between my legs. I shuddered and curled my fingers against his.

When I looked at him, his eyes were closed, whether in ecstasy or pain, I couldn't tell. I moved his palm over my hardening body. Then he moved it, rubbing, and we stumbled out of the chairs and he pushed me against the wall. His hand never left my crotch. I clung to his wrist and began to grind into his palm frantically. His other hand went around my neck, not squeezing, just keeping me pinned to the wall.

"Michael," he whispered. "That's good."

I dared a glance at him. He was watching my body and his hand, watching me rub the front of my jeans furiously against him.

I was going to come like that, but he pulled away.

I went after him automatically. "Please." I touched his face, his neck. He pressed me into the wall again—gently, but firmly—and held me there.

"No," he said. "You don't want to do this. You have a girlfriend. Trust me." He shook me, and then he released me and sat back down.

My erection hurt, it was so tight against my jeans. My knees wobbled. He was right, if he meant that I didn't want to cheat on Nicole, but I only knew one way to make this feeling stop. I touched the front of my pants. Would he watch?

"The bathroom, Michael."

His quiet voice ordered me out, and I obeyed.

3 1

MICHAEL

AFTER WHAT HAPPENED IN THE annex, the only thing to do was leave. I couldn't stay around him—I would try again, and he might not be so forgiving—and I couldn't even think about working on the profile. So I sat by the front door and tied my sneakers clumsily.

He drifted into the room and watched me.

"I'll g-get going," I said.

"Yes, I think you should."

"Can I come back on Monday?"

He didn't answer. My pulse battered against my ribs.

"Can I come back?" I repeated.

I didn't hear his approach, but I felt his fingers sift through my hair.

"Michael," he said with a sigh. I leaned my temple against his knee. The gesture came so naturally.

He crouched and I remained completely still, as if a lion were sniffing at me. His long fingers pushed through my hair, pulling at the strands almost painfully, and he dragged a hand down my spine to my tailbone. He touched my flanks, my chest. It was impossible to tell if he wanted to shove me away or crush me closer. Or just crush me.

The smell of his clean skin and hair filled my nostrils. Finally, I opened my mouth against his jaw and he pushed me back.

"You need to go." He was breathless.

"Monday?" I clung to his shirt.

He disentangled me and walked back to the annex.

32

MICHAEL

I THOUGHT THAT CAL MIGHT text to make sure I got home safe, or maybe to say that I could come back on Monday. He didn't.

I tried to think seriously about what I had done—what it meant about my professionalism or myself—but my brain would not cooperate. All I could think about was how his hand had felt on me, and how he hadn't taken it away. *Michael. That's good.*

He wanted me. I couldn't believe it. He wanted me.

I held on to that idea because it gave me courage.

Nicole was out when I got home, so I waited at the kitchen table and rehearsed what I would say. I remembered Cal's confident tone when he had pushed me into the wall and shaken me. *You don't want to do this. You have a girlfriend. Trust me.*

He knew something about infidelity; I was positive of it.

Furio seemed to sense my anxiety. He whined and paced the kitchen, looked at me expectantly, and finally flopped at my feet, chin on paws. How sad, that the hardest part of breaking up with Nicole would be the logistics: Who got Furio, and where would I live? How would my stream be affected? Who was keeping the new flat screen?

As to the actual relationship, Nicole and I had been over for months. I saw that clearly now. We had become like two friends who barely got along but who happened to live together and were making it work.

We were heading for a dead end, with or without Cal's appearance in my life.

Cal had simply sped things along.

None of that knowledge made it easier, though, when Nicole got home and asked what was wrong. I told her something had happened. I told her we needed to stop being together, living together, because it wasn't working. She panicked. She wanted to know if I had cheated on her, if it was about the sex (or lack thereof), and if there was anything she could do to make me change my mind.

I said no, no, and no, and we held each other and cried.

When she asked if there was someone else, I said no again.

For all I knew, it wasn't a lie.

33

CALEB

I DIDN'T GO TO CHURCH on Sunday. It wouldn't have been appropriate. I knew what I was going to do with Michael, and whenever I know I'm going to sin, I do it anyway and I pretend God doesn't exist.

This habit has always made my guilt and self-loathing worse, but maybe it has also preserved me. Without a little sin in my life, I would have died a long time ago.

Michael arrived on Monday, later than usual, two hours after my run. I was showered and dressed, seated in the family room. When I heard his tires on the drive, I thought, for the second time, *he's like a kicked dog.* My ex-wife's alcoholic uncle had kicked his dog and the poor creature had loved him anyway and came when he was called.

I didn't want to hurt Michael—I wanted to be gentle and good to him—but I wasn't the right person for gentleness and goodness. I hated myself too much to begin to know how to be good to someone else.

But I knew that Michael only wanted me, the same way I only wanted him, and so we were locked together in this cruel situation.

He let himself in on a wave of nervous energy. I had to quietly admire his bravery. It couldn't have been easy, stepping into my house that day.

"Sorry I'm late," he said.

My presence on the couch threw him. He approached, stopped halfway, and looked toward the kitchen. I was usually in the kitchen. He was usually on the couch. I could see the gears spinning in his head. Was he supposed to go to the kitchen?

"Have a seat." I gestured to the cushion beside me. There was no need to keep him at a distance anymore.

He plopped down a few feet away.

"What are you reading?" He glanced at the book on my lap.

"John Muir. Heard of him?"

He shook his head.

"He was an outdoorsman. A conservationist. A little bit of a philosopher, too." I tossed the book onto the coffee table.

"I can see why you'd enjoy that." He focused on his laptop, typing busily.

"You must have pages of notes by now."

"I guess." He stopped typing.

"Any progress on the profile itself?"

"Uh . . . no."

"What is it?"

"Nothing."

I could always tell when he wanted to laugh, or when some awkward thought was crossing his mind. He did a terrible job of concealing his emotions.

"Tell me," I said.

He sank deeper into the cushion and cringed. "When you . . . well, when . . . I mean, I did write one line, on my desktop at home. It was a joke." He couldn't look at me. "It was after our first meeting. After . . . when I thought you fired me."

"Well, now you have to tell me."

He opened and closed his mouth, and then he typed out a line and turned his laptop toward me. At the top of an otherwise blank document were the words *Caleb Bright is a son of a bitch.*

I laughed so hard my eyes watered.

On the edge of my vision, I could see him staring at me like I had sprouted a second head. Apparently, I had been more of a monster than I knew.

"Inspired," I said when I caught my breath.

He smiled apprehensively. "I was mad. It was stupid."

"No, no. I was very rude that day." The humor faded from my expression. I lapsed into thought for a while, about that first meeting with Michael and the ones that followed. "More than that day, really. It was hard for me."

His fingers became very still on the laptop.

"My girlfriend. I'm moving out. I told her."

I looked at him sharply. "Told her what?"

"Oh, not—no. I told her I wanted to end it, that's all. I'd never . . ."

My violin and bow were still on the coffee table. I rose and lifted them and began to pace. "Are you sad? About the breakup."

"Not really." He shrugged. "Three years is a long time, but it hasn't been good for a while. I mean, it was sad to do, but . . . actually saying the words felt like a formality, you know? Like declaring the thing dead." He decompressed visibly as he rambled about the split. He told me how they had agreed on shared custody of the dog, and how he would get most of the appliances because she was keeping the house. It was a relief, he said, and he thought that Nicole, after her initial upset, had seemed relieved, too.

I nodded and listened, moving to and fro.

I wanted to press the tip of the violin bow to his throat and run it down to his navel. My God, he was beautiful.

"Then I'm glad," I said once he had finished speaking. "I didn't want you to do something you would regret."

His head came up. "Do you . . . have experience with that?"

"With regret, or with doing something?" I chuckled and placed the violin under my chin. "Well, either way, we'd be getting ahead of ourselves if we talked about that." I played for a while as a means of distraction. It was easy to lose myself in the sound of the bow singing over the strings, and I didn't want Michael asking more questions about regret. Sometimes, he was much too perceptive.

I played a favorite hymn, "Wondrous Love," and a few secular songs, "Greensleeves," "Hallelujah," and the second movement of Dvořák's *Serenade for Strings*—that last one, shamelessly, for impressive effect. It worked. When I lowered the violin, Michael was staring at me in a trance.

"Come here," I said.

He obeyed, as if I had charmed him out of his basket.

"Do you want to try?" I offered the violin.

"It won't be any good," he mumbled. His chest was rising and falling heavily and I was out of patience. I put down the instrument and reached for him.

"You still have your jacket on." I pushed it off his shoulders. He tried to help, struggling against the canvas-like material, until it fell. He smelled as if he had put some effort into smelling good, and in place of his usual graphic tee he wore a plain black shirt. I brushed a hand across it. "Don't change the way you dress for me."

I got down on my knees very deliberately. I wanted him to know that I wanted this, and that I wasn't acting on a whim.

I kissed him through his jeans and he sucked in a breath. Already, he was completely hard. I cupped his balls and found his head and I mouthed at the shape of his shaft. He stuttered out my name almost immediately.

"What is it?" I sat back on my heels.

"Can I lie down?"

His legs were trembling, his knees locked, and his hands were fisted at his sides. I stood up quickly. Without a word, I climbed the stairs to the loft and he followed.

He stopped beside my bed.

I had to tell him to go ahead before he crawled onto the mattress, then turned over and scooted back awkwardly. Lying down, he looked no more comfortable than he had standing up. He gripped my comforter with both hands, turned aside his head, and squeezed his eyes shut as if he were about to endure torture.

I knelt over his legs, rubbing his crotch. His legs spread slightly and I rubbed deeper into the seam. I watched his face, rapt, as little spasms of pleasure parted his lips and made his eyelids flutter.

"Are you okay?" I said.

He gave a tense nod.

"How is this?" I found his head again and massaged it.

"Good," he gasped.

When I started to undo his jeans, he sat bolt upright.

"You don't have to," he said. "You don't have to do that."

I frowned at him, my brow furrowed. "I want to. You have no idea how much I want to." My hands were burning where I had touched him and saliva was gathering in my mouth. "Michael, I want to," I repeated quietly.

I unzipped his jeans and he reassumed a posture that made him look somewhat in pain. I knew, without a doubt, that I was the first man to do this to him, and that knowledge made me tremble.

I opened his fly enough to get at his boxers—boxers, as if he were a teenager—and pulled out his erection. A surge of shame rolled through me as I lowered my head. I was starved for it. I took him into my mouth and sucked hard and fast, plunging him so deep into my throat that I gagged. He came suddenly, almost instantly, in one thick jet.

He shuddered and pushed himself up again, a mixture of horror and confusion on his face. "I'm s-so sorry. Fuck."

I swallowed and let him slide out of my mouth.

He was shaking his head, his face vividly bright. "I . . . I'm not used to it."

In the way of embarrassment, I don't know which cost him more—coming so quickly or admitting that he wasn't used to oral sex.

"Don't apologize." I tugged down his jeans and boxers, past his hipbones, and began to kiss his pelvis, abdomen, and stomach, breathing in the musk of that private area. I dragged my teeth across his skin and sucked gently, avoiding his sensitive cock. I couldn't control the tremor in my limbs as I moved over him. I pushed his shirt up around his armpits and licked and kissed his chest, kneading with my hands. "Beautiful," I breathed, my nose against his sternum. "Michael . . . so beautiful."

How had his girlfriend kept her hands off of him? And how would I, when we needed to work on the insufferable profile?

He stiffened again. I was kissing his ribs when I felt his arousal prodding at my stomach. I wrapped a hand around him.

"Try to hold it this time," I whispered in his ear. "Try to give me this. Do you understand? I need it for a while."

His eyes drifted open and he nodded.

I went slower the second time, stroking and kissing. I sucked on his balls and licked him up and down. When I took him into my mouth, though, I lost control again, forcing him deep, hard, and fast.

"Please." His voice was ragged. "Cal . . . slow down."

For the first time, he released his death grip on the comforter and touched my hair. I shuddered and eased him out of my mouth.

Saliva and cum rolled down my chin.

A large, sticky patch was growing in my boxer briefs, and my dick was aching, but I liked the pain. I had no intention of gratifying my desire.

"Good," I mumbled. "Pull." I reached up and closed his fingers around a chunk of my hair. He got the message. Whenever I started sucking too hard or fast, he tugged at my scalp. Then I would back off, panting, and pick up again slowly.

We went on like that for as long as he could stand it. I made my throat sore with his head. Every time I gagged on it, he convulsed and yanked at my hair.

Finally, in a strained voice, he said, "I need to now."

I looked up his body and caught him watching. His gaze was unfocused, murky, and sweat glistened on his face. I closed my eyes and made him come.

34

MICHAEL

Cal climbed off of me as soon as my second orgasm finished. He swallowed and licked his lips, but I could still see a streak drying along his jaw. During the slow, exquisite torture of my second blowjob, he had played with me and held my tip against his lips and face so that pre-cum had oozed all over him.

And really, what was that? No woman had ever blown me like that, not ever, and every single woman I had been with had claimed to love doing it. But Cal . . .

I rubbed my face and eyes. Cal, Cal . . . he was a starved animal, shaking the whole time, deep-throating me and then telling me how he needed it.

"I'm going to take a quick shower." His voice brought me back to reality.

I sat up too fast and saw spots—spectral white, flying in every direction.

"I can . . ." I shimmied up my jeans. "Do you, I mean . . ." I tried to get a look at the front of his pants, but he had turned away from the bed.

"I'll only be a few minutes."

"Well, I could . . ." *I could join you. I want to join you. I want to make you come, too.* Those words belonged to a much more mature lover than I. All I seemed capable of doing was seeing spots and forming half-sentences.

Cal leaned over and kissed my forehead where damp skin met damp hair. Somehow, I was sweating more than he was.

"Beautiful," he murmured. I would have found that compliment strange coming from anyone else, but coming from him, it made me feel rare and desired. He padded into the master bathroom and pulled the door shut. The lock clicked—I frowned—and I heard the water running a moment later.

He didn't want company, then. I wondered if he would jerk off. Embarrassment prickled up the back of my neck. Of course he would; he would have to take care of himself. I was probably supposed to touch him, somehow, during our encounter, but I hadn't even thought of it.

My bliss quickly shredded into anxiety. I hopped off the bed and straightened my clothes. He had a standing mirror in the corner of the room. I checked myself over, fixed my hair, and pulled his comforter into shape.

Then I hovered, my hand on the bedpost, until he emerged from the bathroom. Steam rolled out around him. He had a black towel banded low around his waist. Grooves of muscle scored his abs. I looked away. I looked back. He laughed.

"Go downstairs, Michael," he said. "I'll be right down."

"Are you sure?" I scratched the back of my neck. Making an advance was not going to happen, since I couldn't even make my eyes move in the appropriate direction. If he asked, though, or showed me or told me what to do . . .

"Go on."

I shuffled out.

The main area of the house seemed to have changed since my trip to the loft. I swept my eyes over the fine furniture, the plush carpeting and pale hardwood floor in the kitchen. Was I one of Cal's belongings now? Or, having been so close to him, did I own some small part of his life? I touched the violin on the coffee table.

That song he had played, and the way he had looked when he was between my legs, would be forever written in the book of my memory.

He came downstairs a moment later, bringing the smell of soap and clean hair. He must have known how attractive he looked in black. He wore black jeans and a dark cashmere sweater, which was a standard outfit for him.

He saw my fingertips on the violin.

"Liking your chances with that now?"

"Oh, no." I moved away from the instrument. I wouldn't honk and squeal on his violin after he had played such transporting music. "What was that song?"

He knew which one I meant, the last one. "Antonín Dvořák. *Serenade for Strings*, the second movement. Bewitching, right?"

I nodded, watching him stroll into the kitchen.

"I played it to seduce you." He lifted his dark brows. There was a little glimmer of amusement in his eyes, but he didn't smile. "Let's smoke."

And now I was actually invited to smoke, invited out to the sacred deck, and he didn't glower and move off when I sat at the table beside him. I wondered if it would always be this way now, or if I was dreaming.

"You looked good playing it." I stared out at the lake. We sat in such a way that our arms and elbows occasionally brushed and I held my breath every time they did. He had looked angry, playing the song, and passionate.

He smoked in silence.

"Do you mind?" I touched the pack.

He hesitated and then passed me his half-smoked cigarette. "Finish mine." He lit another for himself. "What are you thinking about?"

I was thinking about him sucking me so hard it had almost hurt. "I don't know," I said. "Nothing, really."

"I know what you're thinking about. I'm thinking about it, too." He dragged a hand through his wet hair, which must have felt icy in the October air. He looked pale, his eyes far away. "I made sure it hurt my throat. When you aren't here tomorrow, I want to feel that and remember where you were."

I watched his profile, stupefied.

"Next time, I want you on top, thrusting into my mouth." He laid his forehead in his palm and closed his eyes. "Yeah," he whispered. "That'll be good." His voice had thinned nearly into silence. He seemed paler than he had a moment ago, gray-white.

"Are you okay?"

"Fine." He laughed listlessly. More silence stretched between us, comfortable silence, and then he said, "What is this for you?"

"What?"

"This, all that." He gestured back toward the house. "What is it for you? Are you infatuated with me? Curious?"

I blinked a few times. "No, I . . ."

"You aren't infatuated with me?" he pressed. "With my money and my success and my violin playing?"

I couldn't tell if he was gearing up for anger and I didn't want our good rapport to break so soon. "That's not really fair."

"Curious, then? You've obviously never been with a man."

My face warmed. He ruffled my hair; the gesture only succeeded in making me feel smaller. "What is it to you?" I blurted. "Some sad rehashing of Jamie Foust?"

He stiffened and I instantly wished I could take back the words.

He put out his cigarette and went inside.

I jogged after him. "I'm sorry."

"I'm exhausted. Coffee, I think." He gripped the counter. "Would you make it? There . . ." He gestured toward the coffeemaker and moved to the couch.

I found ground coffee in the cupboard and started a pot, but by the time enough for a cup was ready, Cal was dead asleep. I frowned down at his sprawled figure.

"Cal?" I whispered. Before, he had never napped in my presence. Then again, it wasn't an ordinary day for us.

He looked so pale, though, and eerily motionless. I shook his shoulder gently. Nothing. I held my hand in front of his lips and felt a little gust of breath.

I couldn't help myself—I tucked a stripe of hair behind his ear and ran my fingers over his back. Even in sleep, he seemed invulnerable, silently threatening.

I got my laptop and sat on the floor by the couch, listening to his breaths.

The grandfather clock chimed off three o'clock, then four, then five. I reread all my notes pertaining to the profile. They seemed very silly to me now.

"What are you doing?"

His voice made me jump.

His dark eyes were open, gazing at me intently. I hadn't realized how worried I had been until that moment. I slumped forward and I exhaled. "Hi."

"Michael . . ." His voice was thick with fatigue. He ran his fingers through my hair and down the back of my neck. I relaxed another degree. "Hi."

"Hi," I mumbled again.

He chuckled. "Why are you sitting on the floor?"

"You . . . passed out." I wanted to burrow into his side. He exerted a powerful, magnetic sort of pull, but anxiety and uncertainty repelled me.

"I fell asleep. Look at you." He stroked my neck. "Come here."

He made space on the couch and I flew onto it, curling against his body. I didn't know where to put my hands. I folded my arms between us and lay there self-consciously, relief coursing through me.

He draped an arm over me, his chin in my hair.

"Were you worried?" Amusement tickled at his voice.

"I'm fine."

"Did you sit on the floor this whole time?"

"No." I closed my eyes. "I was just checking on you."

His soft laughter vibrated against me.

"I'm slightly anemic, Michael."

"You are?"

"Yes. It makes me dizzy sometimes. Nothing to worry about." He tucked me closer and kissed the top of my head, and then he sat up and sighed. "I should eat."

"Can I help?" I clambered off the couch and headed for the kitchen. Pressed that close to him, I was getting aroused, and I didn't need that right now.

"Yeah, please. There's spinach . . . in the fridge." He sounded winded and he remained on the couch for a while, hands braced on his knees.

"So this is normal?" I pulled the plastic container out of the fridge.

"Completely. I've been to a doctor. Don't worry."

"I'm not. Just asking." I knew I was lying terribly, but my pride could only take so much punishment. Earlier, he had put his mouth on me and I had exploded spontaneously. I winced at the memory. Now, he had caught me sitting on the floor like a dog while he napped, and I was making him food. "What do I do with this?"

"Dressing, put it in a bowl. Get yourself something, too." He was watching me. "What's the matter?"

"Feels funny, cooking for you."

He laughed. "First of all, you're not cooking. And second, trust me, I would rather be doing it. Dizzy, though."

"No, I'm happy to help." I packed a bowl with spinach leaves and sprinkled balsamic dressing over the top. For myself, I found Honey Bunches of Oats.

Cal prayed quickly, head lowered and eyes closed, like he did before every meal.

When I moved to sit at the far end of the table, he smirked and nudged out the chair beside his. I shifted over to it without looking at him.

"Thank you," he said. Beneath the table, he gripped my thigh for a moment. "If I weren't so tired . . ."

I almost spit out my cereal. "No worries." I leaned over the bowl. If he wasn't so tired, what? I imagined him under the table and then I had to stop imagining it.

For a while, the only sounds were our utensils, cereal crunching, and the clock. I watched his forearms. He had pushed up the sleeves of his sweater and I could see the fine dark hairs shading his skin. Blue veins forked over the tops of his hands. He wore a heavy silver watch and a stray hair tie stretched around his wrist.

I could have observed him like that for the rest of the evening.

"About Jamie," he said quietly.

I would have sworn that the temperature dropped. I shook my head and stabbed at my soggy cereal. "You don't have to. I'm sorry. That wasn't appropriate."

"No, it was. How much do you know?"

"Nothing, really. I saw a tiny picture. I know he . . . passed away."

"Sure." Cal nodded slowly.

"Your sister—"

"Yes, I know she mentioned him." He laid down his fork. "She knew him, sort of. We all went to the same camp in the summers."

"Camp Apache?" I remembered the name from my notes.

"The investigative journalist hard at work." A trace of cynicism got into his voice.

"I'm sorry. I only Googled him."

"It does not matter." The words came out gradually, as if he had to force each one. He took a deep breath and shrugged. "It was a Christian camp. We were campers when we met. We were ten, and we both failed the swimming test and had to take lessons for one of our activities. So we were instant friends. I've never had patience for a large social circle. At camp, he and I were . . ." He gestured. "You know, two inseparable friends."

Some color had returned to his face, yet his expression was stricken. He carried our dishes to the sink. I wanted to repeat that he didn't have to tell the story—it caused him such obvious pain—but I was too curious, and too selfish. Jamie Foust and I looked alike. In Cal's world, we were linked. I needed to know how.

"We went every summer for two weeks. We exchanged a few letters between summers. We started working on staff when we were old enough. Seventeen. We were both seventeen then. We worked in the kitchen. I'd lifeguard for some retreats. It was a good place, a good atmosphere. We'd work there all summer, basically."

I tried to picture seventeen-year-old Cal at summer camp. Maybe a happier Cal. Maybe a less intimidating Cal, though I doubted that.

"I need a cigarette," he said.

I followed him outside and stood at the railing while he paced and smoked.

"We were best friends, like I said. Most of the guys on staff were . . . preoccupied with the girls. And the girls were preoccupied with the guys. Everyone sort of paired off. Teens in the summer." He waved a hand, trailing smoke. "Jamie and I spent all our free time together. We got along, you know? Same humor, I guess. We'd fish and hike in our free time, or play music. The staff kids snuck out at night a lot, pranking or going off to sit by the lake. Jamie and I used to hike out to this place in the woods, Council Rock. We'd steal sodas from the kitchen and go out there, make a fire. I'm sure you can see where this is going."

"Tell me anyway," I said. "Please. I don't want to guess."

He lit another cigarette and paused at the railing. "Fine." The way he looked out toward the mountains, I knew he was seeing into the past. "We were walking back from there. It was late. We were being silly, shoving each other. I think I pushed him down. We were wrestling, that's all. He tried to kiss me."

He stopped speaking and stayed quiet, as if the rest were self-explanatory.

"What happened?" I edged closer.

"I punched him in the mouth."

If not for Cal's pained expression, I would have laughed. *I punched him in the mouth*. He said it so matter-of-factly.

"He just . . . wouldn't let me go. I split his lip and he was bleeding. But he knew." He exhaled softly. "He knew what was going on before I did."

"Did you . . . hit him again?"

"No, thank God. We kept fighting, sort of wrestling, only . . . well, I see what we were doing now. We were trying to get off. Kids, you know."

I didn't know. My first sexual encounter had been a sloppy situation after a college party. I envied Cal his wrestling in the woods. However juvenile it seemed to him, it sounded infinitely purer than my drunken encounter with a drunken girl.

"Did you?" I had to keep urging him on now. He was lost in memory.

"Oh, no. We were close enough to the camp that we got spooked. We did later, though. Another night. No more punching. Some wrestling."

"The same way?"

He finally glanced at me. A column of ash fell from his cigarette. "You don't want all the vulgar details, do you?"

I looked away. "Yeah, I do."

"Hm." He grazed a knuckle over my hot cheek, and then he resumed his vigil. "Yes, the same way, at first. Rubbing together through our pants. It seems stupid now, but . . . we were virgins. Half the time, I was finishing in my boxers, and I know he was, too. We did other things, eventually."

"Like what?" I struggled for a nonchalant tone.

He thought for a moment. "The same thing, skin to skin." He was trying to put it delicately. "And what I did to you earlier."

"You did that to him?"

"We did it to each other."

"I can do that, you know," I said in a rush.

I became aware of him watching me again. "Oh?"

"Yeah." I nodded resolutely. Jamie had done it for him. I could do it, too. I even wanted to, sort of, though I knew I would somehow embarrass myself.

"Doesn't the idea disgust you?" He gripped my jaw and made me look at him. The pad of his thumb passed over my lips, which parted instinctively. My heart began to gallop. Was he going to make me do it now?

"D-disgust me?"

"It's one thing to have a man's mouth on you, Michael, and quite another to have it in your mouth."

He really knew how to calm a guy down.

"You seem to . . . do okay."

"That's because I like it. I'm all twisted around inside." He released my jaw. "Anyway, don't worry. I don't want that."

I swallowed and resisted the urge to rub my mouth. My lips were tingling, over-sensitized by his touch. I looked down at my scuffed Vans. He didn't want that. He had let Jamie do it, but he didn't even want me to try. Disappointment and a strong sense of inadequacy swept over me.

"Sure thing," I said.

Apparently, I had met someone who wanted to blow me and get nothing in return. We should all be so lucky, right? But he was robbing me of the chance to give him pleasure, and I wanted to do that. I wanted to know what that felt like.

"These things are the worst when I'm dizzy." He stubbed out his cigarette. "Such a guilty pleasure, though."

We went back inside. I felt that I had been distanced from him, pushed away again, on an intimate level. If he noticed my declining mood, he ignored it.

35

CALEB

Michael tried to steer the conversation back to Jamie, but I shut it down. "Enough about that today," I said, because my heart was aching.

"I look like him," he said.

"You do. It's uncanny."

"Is that why you like me?" He shoved his hands in his pockets and walked toward the family room. He was trying to be big and brave, or some imagined version of mature. "I don't care if that's the reason. It makes sense."

"That's part of it, Michael. That was part of it, at first." I moved up behind him and laid a hand on his shoulder. "But I see you, who you are. You, not Jamie. It was you I wanted to take to bed today."

He curled in on himself whenever I spoke about anything sexual. I felt his shoulders drawing together and he folded his arms across his chest. It made me want him more, that timidity. I knew it wouldn't last forever. I would be the one to crush it; he would come for me so many times that all his bashfulness would wear away. For now, though, it was incredibly alluring.

And it made his onset of sadness difficult to understand. I had told him that I didn't want him to suck me off. That should have been a relief, given his crippling shyness. Instead, he had taken the news like a blow.

I settled in an armchair and watched him, wondering. Did he really want to do it, or was he competing with the ghost of Jamie?

Ah, Jamie . . . he had wanted to do it. I closed my eyes and remembered the first time, his tongue on me there, the sun falling in bars around us.

"Cal?"

I opened my eyes. It was a shock to my system to see Michael standing there, looking so much like Jamie.

"Are you feeling okay?"

I smiled placidly. "Yes." It wasn't a lie. I had cut too deep during my shower and blood had filled the bottom of the tub in a diffuse red sheet. I had spent most of my time in the bathroom trying to staunch the bleeding, and when I had finally bandaged and taped the wound, my dick was soft and my head was in the clouds.

Dangerous . . . I had passed out.

I liked riding that crumbling edge, though. Everything was in a mist.

"Are you dizzy?"

"Only a little. Let's make a fire." By that, I meant let me watch you make a fire, and he obliged because his chronic anxiety made him restless.

He had slipped off his sneakers by the deck door. His socks looked relatively new, as did his shirt. He had probably imagined me undressing him today. I smiled to myself.

Under the full force of my attention, his nervousness tripled. He dropped a log, swore. The chain curtain caught, then lurched open, and he jumped.

"Would telling you to relax have any effect?"

He smirked. "Probably a negative effect, to be honest."

"Then relax." I laughed. "This is entertaining."

"You're kind of a dick."

"Caleb Bright is a son of a bitch," I quipped.

He snickered and shook his head. Soft pieces of hair flopped across his brow, into his eyes. I gazed at his body openly. He was thin, but not gaunt—proportionate and smooth-skinned—and so sensitive I would swear no one had ever touched him.

After he lit the fire, he knelt on the carpet and watched the flames. I thought about so many things—his mouth on me, or telling him to relax before I took him from behind—and then I climbed over him, pressing him into the carpet.

"Relax," I whispered in his ear.

I stroked him through his pants. When he tried to unbutton them, I pinned his wrists above his head.

"Cal," he panted urgently. "I need to . . ."

I told him to relax again, I told him it was okay, and I rubbed until he came in his boxers. As soon as I released his hands, he scrambled back.

He glared at me and rubbed his wrists.

"Why the hell did you do that?" he snapped.

"Because I wanted to," I answered simply. "Because I want you to think about me while you're driving home, and now you'll have to, won't you?"

36

MICHAEL

It was difficult to leave that day, but after what Cal had done to me, I didn't have much choice. He seemed to get no end of pleasure out of watching me adjust my jeans and walk uncomfortably to my laptop. He returned to his armchair and grinned wickedly, jaw in palm, dark eyes trailing me around the room.

"I would have thought about you anyway," I muttered.

"I prefer it this way. I'll be thinking about it, too."

The back of my neck was on fire.

"It'll dry and press against you," he added.

"You're crazy." I snagged my computer and went to lace up my shoes. No matter how I stood or sat, the damp patch in my boxers made itself known.

I wasn't really angry, though. I was embarrassed and aroused. Still, I found myself envying Jamie again, who had gotten Cal when they were both naïve.

I tugged on my jacket and loitered by the front door.

"Well," I said.

He remained seated, gazing at me. Now it was just getting awkward. I had half-expected him to walk me out, something he had only done when I had barged in on his sister, or maybe to kiss me, which was ridiculous, because he hadn't kissed me on the mouth all day. Maybe he didn't do mouth kisses. No big deal. I wasn't so sentimental that I wanted a kiss goodbye, right?

"Are you okay over there, Michael?"

I was Michael to him, always, never Mike. I liked that.

"I'm fine. I'll see you Wednesday?"

"Wednesday." He moved two fingers in a diminutive wave.

Cal's stunt by the fireplace worked as intended. I thought about him the whole way home: His mouth and hands, his arms, eyes, voice. Leaving the mountains, I felt that I was returning to reality from a dream. None of that could have been real and I wouldn't let myself hope to replicate the experience.

I streamed for half a day on Tuesday, throwing myself into end-over-end competitive Overwatch matches, and as I was winding down, I got a new subscriber (*cbsonofab*) and a one hundred dollar donation from the same, no message. My face flushed in front of five thousand viewers.

"Oh, damn. CB dropping the brand new sub *and* top dono of the day right at the end of the stream. Guys, can we get some hot mics and drop the mics in the chat please?" He was watching my stream. I shifted in my chair. "Dang, dude. That's huge. Thank you so much. Not even leaving a message, just dropping the mic and walking away."

During my stream, I had a running (and highly chauvinistic) joke that involved telling the top donator of the day that he had "the biggest dick in the chat." Whenever I received a large donation or when a viewer topped the day's largest donation, I would make a speech about how the donator had the hugest dick/wiener/schlong. But I was not doing that for Cal. I couldn't possibly say it without stumbling all over myself, and he already got too many laughs at my expense.

"What a great way to end the stream," I said quickly, bowing my head toward the webcam. "Thanks for the insane support today, guys. If it's your first time here and you liked what you saw, don't forget to hit that follow button. And, I'm out bros. Keep an eye on Twitter for schedule updates. Things are a little up in the air lately with real life stuff, but I'll be back to my regular schedule soon. Peace."

I played my outro and pushed away from the desk.

Seconds later, a text from Cal pinged on my phone. **Where's my big dick speech? Unsub/unfollow.**

He had caught on to the mores of Twitch chat, and my channel in particular, with alarming speed.

I thought for a while before replying. It was much easier to joke around via text. **I wouldn't really know about that, now would I?**

I waited for a response that never came.

Jk, I added a few minutes later.

Still, he was silent.

I frowned at Furio. "Dude, I made a dick size joke and he's not answering." Furio cocked his head, oblivious to my human troubles. What if Cal wasn't big or even average? What if, improbably, he was small and self-conscious about it? I buried my face in my hands. "I'm an idiot."

I didn't care about his size, but he would care, of course.

Hell, if he was on the small side, it might make a few things easier . . .

"No," I said aloud, abruptly. "I'm not thinking about this."

I spent the rest of the day thinking about it and packing my belongings into boxes and totes. And checking my phone, which was silent.

I would sign the lease for my new apartment on Thursday and start driving over loads on the weekend. I had a few friends with trucks, but I didn't want to tell them about the breakup. I hadn't even told my parents yet. They liked Nicole, and they liked seeing me semi-settled. In their eyes, breaking up and moving out would be a regression.

I woke much too early on Wednesday, at four thirty, and with that distinct alertness that will not be lulled back to sleep. I had been relegated to the couch until my move, but the couch wasn't to blame for my early waking. No, I was looking forward to seeing Cal, and I was subconsciously worried about our texts.

Once upon time, Nicole had told me that I overanalyzed things "like a girl." Maybe she was right, though I suspect overthinking isn't specific to one gender.

Whatever the case, I kept wondering what Cal had been trying to accomplish with his text yesterday—if he was flirting or missing me, or just teasing me—and how and why my response had silenced him.

I made up my improvised bed and put on coffee. Furio emerged from Nicole's room, slow blinking, to assess the situation, but even he wasn't interested in being up at that hour. He curled up on the warm spot I had left on the couch.

I checked my e-mail, brainstormed a new blog post, and then, with three cups of coffee pumping through me, I did the unthinkable. I put on basketball shorts and a hoodie and I went for a jog.

I barely made it around our small block, but I staggered back to the house feeling enormously proud. Nicole was up by then and she stared at me like I was a home invader.

"How long have you been awake?" Her voice was chilly. I could hear the suspicion in it. For three years, she had tried to motivate me to work out, and suddenly we were breaking up and I was running of my own volition.

"Too long," I said. "Not sure what gives."

I headed to the bathroom before she could ask what she really wanted to ask.

In the hope of lasting a few seconds longer if Cal touched me today, I rubbed one out in the shower. I thought about him.

I thought about the question he had asked when I had clumsily offered to blow him. *Doesn't the idea disgust you?*

The answer was no, unequivocally.

He had told me not to change the way I dressed, so I wore a *Game of Thrones* T-shirt that said *Crows Before Hoes*. It seemed comically appropriate, and since we had watched the series together, I knew he would get it.

I gunned it to Red Feather and arrived a few minutes before eleven.

Cal was walking out of the annex as I let myself in. The clean, chemical odor of paint trailed him. His hair was tied back and dark lounge pants hung from his hips.

"You'll never believe what I did this morning," I said.

He approached, unsmiling, and I flattened myself against the door.

I was learning to recognize that particular look on his face.

His hand closed around my throat, compressing the airway until only a thread of breath could pass. Then he practically stood on top of me. His legs and knees pushed at mine, and his stomach and chest and shoulders. He must have felt my thundering heart.

"Is this big enough for you?" he hissed. He grasped my free hand and pressed it between his legs. The thin fabric of his pants stretched over his erection, and he was thick and long, unnervingly so.

Not small, then.

Not even average.

I closed my watering eyes and pulled in as much air as I could.

"Do you want that down your throat?"

I couldn't reply and he knew it. I could barely breathe. Still, I tried to stroke him.

His fingers tightened.

For one vertiginous moment, I wondered if he knew what the hell he was doing, and the thought that he might actually have killed Jamie Foust flashed through my mind.

He released my neck and I sagged against him.

"It was a joke," I panted.

But it was not a joke to Cal, apparently. He gripped my arm and dragged me upstairs. I went willingly enough, though I was shaking. The loft was dark. He slid my laptop onto a chair and he undressed me brusquely, yanking off my sneakers and socks, jeans, boxers, jacket, and shirt, until I stood naked in front of him.

He shoved me and I tumbled onto the comforter, and then he was on top of me, kissing me hard, biting my lips and tugging at my hair. "Michael," he gasped. "Michael."

Our bodies brushed, there, and I realized he had taken his cock out of his pants.

My heels dug into the mattress. I rubbed my length along his again and he moaned. I had wanted to hear that so badly—to make him do that.

"Take off my shirt," he said.

I dragged it over his head and clung to his shoulders. I wanted to reach between us, to feel him. Why couldn't I make my hands go there? Tentatively, I moved my palms across his arms and back. He was rigid all over.

He reached for something on the bedside table, and then he lifted his hips enough to spread warm, glossy fluid over my shaft.

"God," he whispered. "Now. Like this."

We rubbed together steadily, our erections sliding and bumping. I needed to come within moments and he seemed to know it. He slowed down, almost stopped. My fingers were biting into his ribs.

"Do you need to come?" His voice was strained.

I nodded, my eyes pinched shut.

"Do it then, Michael." He started to move again. "Come on me." The band of his lounge pants kept pressing against my balls, creating a different sort of friction. He knew just how to move to make the bell of his head catch on mine again and again. His hair had come loose. It hung over my face, teasing my skin. I tasted sweat, smelled firewood. When I cracked open my eyes, I saw him pumping over me, his chest, his arms, his breath was in my hair, and I came with a groan.

Afterward, he kissed my mouth. It was easier, then, to wind my arms around his neck and raise my belly to his.

He rolled me onto my side and moved behind me. My eyes flew open. He was still hard, resting along the cleft of my backside. I went completely still. "Cal . . ."

"On your stomach," he murmured, pushing me down.

My heart pounded against the bed.

He settled on top of me and pressed my legs together. I must have looked pathetic, shaking and clinging to a pillow.

"Tight," he said.

I didn't understand until his shaft plunged between my thighs. I jolted with relief. He held the back of my neck and gripped my hair as he thrust. I squeezed my legs together tighter and tried to raise my hips so that his head didn't grind against the bed.

He wasn't gentle with me. I liked that. I bucked into the force of his body, feeling his strength and mine, and he held me down and drove against me. When he came, he bit my shoulder so hard that I knew his teeth would leave a mark.

Most of his cum ended up on the bed, but some of it flecked my abs. I reached down and touched it, I don't know why, except that it made me overwhelmingly happy, knowing he had done it with me.

37

CALEB

My heart rushed in my ears like the ocean in a shell. Poor, terrified Michael, all my desire had broken against him. At least I hadn't hurt him. At least I hadn't forced him into something painful and wrong.

I pulled up my pants and rolled off of him. I stared at the ceiling, my chest rising and falling. A light sweat clung to my skin.

"Why are you apologizing?" He sat up and hugged his legs.

"Was I?" I said.

"Yeah . . . just now."

I looked over at him and only then did I realize I had stripped him completely. He was shivering and trying to hide most of his body. I sat up and kissed his shoulder.

"Don't hide."

He shook his hair out of his eyes. "I'm not."

But he was—he was hiding his chest with his arms, his soft penis with the bend of his leg, his ass against the comforter. I made him lie down.

He was always pliant, except a moment ago when I had humped into his legs. He had fought me then, struggling against my arms, which was how I liked it.

I looked him over, up and down. He closed his eyes while I did.

"I missed you," I said. "That's all. I didn't mean to frighten you."

"I'm fine. Really."

If he could have seen himself shaking.

"Roll over," I said, nudging him onto his stomach. I pushed his legs apart and gazed at his tapered back, his ass, his balls, the lube still shining between his thighs. I massaged his back for a while.

He finally found his voice. "I thought you were mad about the text."

"No." I kneaded down the sides of his spine. "But you made a fair point, and I wanted you to know . . ."

"Know what?"

I wasn't sure how to articulate the feeling, which was rare for me. I brushed my fingers over his ass and watched him shift uncertainly. "That my body is . . . good," I said a bit lamely. "For you, I mean. That you can . . . I don't know. That it's not bad. That it's worth your time. Does that make sense?"

His eyes were wide and he had become very still. "Are you kidding me?" A muscle in his thigh trembled. "Your body is perfect."

"Flattery will get you everywhere with me." I tilted my head and brushed my thumb over his anus. He held his breath and achieved an even more sincere, Zen-like level of stillness. Only the puckered skin under my thumb moved, tightening in response to my touch. "Are you all right?"

"Fine," he whispered.

I kept flickering my finger over him there, watching him.

"Do you like this?"

"I don't know." His voice was barely audible. "I think so."

I smirked and climbed off the bed. Too much of that, and we would never be finished. "You can clean up in the bathroom."

I walked into my closet and waited to hear the bathroom door shut before changing. The cuts on my inner thighs—two on one side, one on the other—were an ugly, angry red. I pulled on boxer briefs, black jeans, and a pale, cabled sweater.

When I stepped out, Michael was hopping into his jeans beside my bed. I stared at him for a beat. "You know that blog post you wrote about your dog—how he can't look serious doing anything?"

He stopped mid-pant-hop and laughed. "You're a dick."

I chuckled and handed him his shirt. "I hope you know I'm kidding. Don't worry, you looked very serious a few minutes ago."

"Dude, you make me really self-conscious." He pulled on his shirt. *Dude.* He was getting more comfortable with me. "I can't believe you'd ever be worried about your body. That's crazy to me."

"You're attracted to me?"

He glared mildly and carried his laptop downstairs. "Don't make it weird."

"I'm serious. Are you attracted to me, or to men in general?"

"You," he answered promptly. "Yeah . . . you. I don't know." He rubbed his jaw and contemplated the floor. His seeming lack of self-awareness bewildered me. "I guess there could be someone else, but that's hard to imagine right now. What about you?"

"Oh, very attracted to myself, for sure." I stepped outside and lit a cigarette. He followed quickly.

"You know what I mean."

"I'm not gay, if that's what you're asking. I have no use for labels like that. It was Jamie, first, and now you."

He tried, and failed, to conceal his surprise. "No one else?"

"You two, my ex-wife."

"Three partners?" He was looking at me skeptically.

"Michael, I'm a Christian." I wanted to cuff him on the back of the head, give him something to really look surprised about. "Yes, three. And that's two too many."

I could tell he wanted to say more about that, but whatever it was, he decided against it. He nodded a little and went quiet.

"I'm sure you've had more," I said.

"Well, yeah." He laughed reluctantly. "Which is insane. You could be a model."

"You have to stop flirting with me." I cupped the side of his face. "I can't focus. Do you understand? We'll never get anything done."

Desire did something very particular to his eyes—it gave him a heavy-lidded, hazy stare—and it made his lips part. "Sorry."

He was slowly driving me insane.

"Please, try to look sorry." I walked away.

"Would you tell me more about Jamie?"

There—that was a sufficient mood-killer. I lit a second cigarette. "Oh. Where did we leave off?"

"You two at camp. You were seventeen."

"Right." I hadn't forgotten. I needed time to go back to those memories, though. "Ah, he wasn't there the next summer. He was taking summer courses, for college. He was at a school out here, actually." I gestured generally to the landscape.

"Here? In Colorado?"

"Right. He invited me to visit that summer. He had his own dorm room." I brushed my fingers over the railing. "My parents let me go. Everyone thought we were great friends, nothing else. We started having sex then. It was his idea—he wanted to. Of course, I wanted it too. I was still a virgin. We both were."

Michael fidgeted with his coat.

"What is it?" I frowned at him. I could easily guess.

"I'm curious, I mean, who—"

"I was on top. But I was more nervous than he was, somehow. I was shaking. He had a few beers. I didn't want any. I really didn't drink back then, and I was worried I might not be able to . . . you know." I felt my eyes clouding with memory. "God, I was young. I'll never be that nervous again. I'll never get that back."

"How was it?" He was almost whispering.

"Oh, good." I nodded faintly. "It was good. Pandora's Box sort of thing. We couldn't stop, after that." I cleared my throat and tried to shake off the memory: Jamie's shoebox of a dorm room, the twin mattress, the way I had kept asking if it hurt and the way he kept reaching back, grasping my hip, telling me to do it to him.

He had wanted it again the next day, though he must have been sore. And the next day, and the next. Sometimes, we had barely made it back to his room.

"Cal?"

"What?" This time, I knew not to look at Michael so immediately after surfacing from memory. He was the ghost of my first lover and it frightened me.

"Did you see him the next summer?"

"Oh, no. It was over then. I worked one more summer on staff. I e-mailed him a few times, but I didn't hear back. I figured he was fighting it. I didn't want to interfere with that. And anyway, I was busy with school, and then Coral happened."

"Okay."

I gripped the deck and closed my eyes. One more installment and I would be done revisiting the way I had ruined our lives. "That's enough for now, I think."

"That's fine." He touched my arm. I knew it took superhuman amounts of courage for him to touch me, but the timing was wrong. I shook off his hand and grimaced.

"It's disgusting, honestly," I said. "Two men behaving like that. It's so obviously unnatural. God puts these obstacles in our lives to test us, and he never presents us with a challenge we can't overcome. I just chose to fail. I choose to fail."

Whenever I talked about spiritual matters, Michael became intensely silent and looked at me as if I were speaking Russian. He had no basis for understanding faith. From what I could tell, he had been raised by Berkeley hippies, transplanted in Boulder, and brought up in the *do what makes you happy/all roads lead to Rome* school of faith.

"You're such a millennial." I moved inside and he followed like a puppy. "Your whole generation is psychologically incapable of accepting a higher power."

"Aren't you a millennial, too?" He laughed uneasily.

"I'd rather not class myself as that."

"Don't take this the wrong way"—he gravitated toward his laptop—"but your God sounds kind of . . . scary. And harsh."

"He is, Michael."

"Why would you want to worship that?"

"You act like there's some other god available."

"Well, why have any god?" He ducked onto the couch. "Why not make up your own mind about things?"

I simmered in silence for a while. *Make up your own mind.* That was the rhetoric of Michael's disoriented generation. I had unshakable faith in God's existence, though, passed down through my family from as far back as we could trace our ancestry. I knew that the Bible, in its consistency and historicity, was like no other religious text, and I had studied it in Hebrew and Greek, and I believed its every word. I knew what I believed. It comforted me to know. And when I looked at people like Michael, making up rules for themselves as they went along, and foolishly hoping for the best, I felt sorry for them.

"I'm not like you," I finally said, withdrawing into myself. At least, with Jamie, there had been a common denominator of faith. We had known that what we were doing was wrong. Michael's atheism—or agnosticism, or whatever it was—made me feel, at times, more alone than ever.

38

MICHAEL

CAL DIDN'T FINISH THE STORY of Jamie until the end of October. Our meetings, and his moods, were up and down. Nearly every time I arrived at his house, he took me straight to bed. He would usually blow me, but on occasion he would undress halfway and we would rub together. I liked that best. It felt closer to sex. He would kiss me and moan my name, and sometimes he would let me jerk him to climax.

Whenever I finished him like that, he propped himself up and watched.

Often, during oral sex, he would arrange himself so that I could thrust into his mouth. Sometimes, he liked to watch me jerk off. He would tell me where to touch myself and how. He always knew what he wanted, but whereas I felt alive and exultant in our intimacy, Cal seemed like an animal caught in barbed wire. His dark eyes were haunted, even at the height of passion. The more he struggled for release, the deeper some private pain cut into him. I could guess that it was guilt—he made no secret of his conservative views—but I knew there had to be more to it, a personal vein.

I only tried to take off his boxer briefs once. We were moving together and I wanted to feel his whole, bare body against mine. I hooked my thumbs under his waistband and he flung back my wrists so violently that they struck the headboard. It hurt, and I didn't try again.

He didn't come that day. He had a habit of finishing me and then disappearing, unsatisfied, into the shower. I was never invited. He would emerge, fifteen to twenty minutes later, looking pale and dazed. I theorized that he had a secret drug problem. Once, I rummaged through his bathroom drawers and cabinet, confident that I would find needles or pills. Instead, I found toilet paper, cleaning and first aid supplies, over-the-counter medications, a shaving kit, a pocketknife, a pair of shears.

I finally decided that nakedness, and sometimes even coming, were limits for Cal, somehow related to sex. Pandora's Box: An irrevocable unleashing of evil. That was how Cal had described sex with Jamie, and he didn't want to go there with me. But as weeks passed, the days with him and then the days without him, I began to crave that closeness and to fantasize about it.

I wasn't trapped in Cal's Christian guilt. I wasn't even personally conflicted by our relationship. I could hardly believe that once I had envied Cal's silver spoon upbringing, because now I saw that it was more like a silver cage, and I was so thankful for my parents and the way they had raised me. I was free.

Each day, after we fooled around and got cleaned up, I would try to work on the profile. I prepared questions and discussion topics ahead of time, as it was increasingly difficult to think in his presence.

Mysteriously, I had the same effect on him.

"My hands need to be busy when you're around," he said, so he would paint or cook or fiddle with a guitar as we talked about his life and work. We also walked around the lake and through the groves of aspen and lodge pole pines on his property.

By then, I was fully settled in my new apartment in Superior, and I invited him over on the last weekend in October. He said yes, to my surprise, and drove down himself.

The simple fact of his driving to my place, instead of the usual reverse, set me on edge. I cleaned and re-cleaned and sat on the couch and looked out the window.

He arrived at noon with a bottle of expensive bourbon.

"Housewarming gift," he explained, striding in and immediately making the place feel smaller. He set the bottle in the kitchen and looked around. "This is nice, Michael."

It *was* a nice apartment, quite new, with high ceilings, soft gray walls, hardwood floors, and stylish, modern fixtures. I would have been lying if I said I hadn't chosen the apartment with him in mind, and with a view to owning someplace mature, adult.

I smiled and opened the bourbon. "Thanks. I like it a lot. Drink?"

He nodded.

We barely drank together anymore, which meant that he had been using alcohol, early on, to make being around me bearable.

I poured us two generous glasses.

Today, it was my turn to need it.

"Oh, are we getting drunk?" He laughed and accepted the glass.

"Why not?" I took a gulp.

He eyed me thoughtfully before taking a sip. "Show me around."

There wasn't much to show. The kitchen area opened into the family room, and down the hall was my office with my streaming setup, the laundry room, bathroom, and bedroom. Furio was with Nicole that weekend.

He grinned at the treadmill in my bedroom. "Wonders never cease."

"I've been running thirty minutes a day. Trying to . . . get healthier."

"I thought your thighs seemed a little stronger." He touched my leg.

I backed into the door and drained my glass. "Thanks."

"Is everything all right?" He frowned.

"Yeah. There's a deck, too." I hurried back to the kitchen to refill my glass. Cal had barely dented his drink and was now watching me with open suspicion.

I showed him the small deck. I had put two chairs there and a chiminea.

"Smoking amenities," he said. "I approve."

"Do you want to smoke?"

"No, I want to know what's the matter with you."

"Nothing. Really."

"Don't lie to me." His eyes narrowed. "Am I making you nervous, being here? I can leave." He moved back inside and set his glass on the counter.

I downed my second drink and followed him.

"No, that's—no. I want you here." I had imagined this going differently, but I should have known better. He could always see right through me. "I want to show you something." On cue, my heart began to leap like it was trying to escape up my throat.

"Show me, then," he said tersely.

I nodded and walked to the bedroom, aware of him trailing. I peeled off my shirt, took a deep breath, and kissed his neck.

"Michael, did you get some kind of alarming tattoo?" His voice was already husky, the anger gone. He gripped my hips and rolled back his head.

"No." My hands trembled as I lifted his sweater.

That day, thank God, he raised his arms and let me take off his top. I kissed his chest and he sighed.

"A piercing?"

"No." I backed toward the bed, pushing down my pants as I did. My face was already furiously hot. "It's something . . . I've been trying." I stepped out of my boxers and lay back on the bed, closing my eyes. That helped—blocking out the sight of him standing there, staring down at me.

I bent my knees and gripped my stiff length. Before I could talk myself out of it, I sucked on my index finger, reached down, and pressed it into my bottom. Cal made a soft, strangled noise. I felt the mattress shift, his hands parting my thighs.

"Show me," he whispered.

I stroked myself and slid my finger in and out.

"God, Michael. Let me . . ." He brushed my hands away from my body. I squeezed the quilt as his finger, slick with saliva and longer than mine, wriggled into me. My spine bowed off the bed. I opened my eyes and gazed at him.

"Is this what you want?" He fingered me and pumped my cock slowly. When I shook my head, he added a second finger and moved them faster, harder. I started to shake. Drops of cum oozed onto my belly.

"More," I managed.

His eyes were molten, his mouth slack. He twisted me over abruptly, his fingers pulling out of me so fast that it hurt. I raised my ass. As if I could make my wishes any clearer, I gripped one of my cheeks and spread it to the side.

His tongue plunged into me—a sensation so unexpected and illicit that I groaned and pushed against his mouth. I clung to my pillow, my jaw clenching and loosening, my thighs quaking. "Cal, please . . . more."

At last, then, he caught my meaning. His tongue withdrew. "That's what you want," he said. His voice was low and cautious. It wasn't a question.

I took the bottle of lubricant from my bedside table drawer, tossed it back onto the quilt, and lowered my head.

"I know you've never asked," I said, "but I have . . . papers. I've been tested. You could see them any time."

He was quiet.

I glanced back.

He had the bottle in his hand, but he was just staring at it.

My two large drinks were finally hitting me, making my limbs loose and my head light. "I'm losing my fucking mind," I told him, "wanting it."

"I don't care about the tests," he said after a while. "I never did." That small, disturbing statement made the hair on my neck stand up. "I've been with two virgins and you." He was taking off his pants. I closed my eyes again and listened to the sound of him stroking lubricant onto himself.

"I trust you," I said.

He spread lube onto me and into me. I rocked back on his finger a few times.

"Michael," he whispered when he pressed his tip to my ass. "Relax . . ."

I didn't care about relaxing, though. I pushed back, forcing him in, and told him to do it. The sound he made was half pleasure, half pain. I began shaking so badly that I had to lie flat on the bed. He slid all the way in, until I felt his balls. It frightened me—that thick rod inside of me, pinning me down—and I couldn't move for fear.

"Tell me I'm the first to fuck you." He shifted his hips in a subtle, circular motion, as if letting me know who was in control. I felt the motion deep in my body.

"You're the first . . . to fuck me." A tear leaked out of my eye. It wasn't from passion or pain. It came, I think, from relief.

"Do you still want this?" He brushed the hair away from my face, pulled halfway out of me, and thrust back in.

"Yes," I whispered, shuddering.

39

MICHAEL

"Did I hurt you?" Cal tugged up his jeans and sprawled beside me. I remained belly down on the quilt, a damp patch beneath me. I hadn't expected to come—not from that—but the fear, the pressure of his penis filling me, and the friction of mine against the quilt had accomplished it. Cal had come a heartbeat later, inside of me.

I pushed sweaty hair from my eyes and gazed tranquilly at his bicep. I had no wish to move for the foreseeable future.

"Michael?" Concern laced his voice.

"I'm fine. I'm good."

"Did it hurt?" He ran a hand down my spine.

I had to think about the question for a moment. "A little," I said. "But I liked it. I didn't really try to relax."

"I noticed." He eased me onto my side and spotted my mess. A bewildered look crossed his face, and then he smirked. "Would a steady breeze get you off?"

I laughed fitfully. "It was . . . the quilt."

"Oh, it was the quilt?" He laughed, too, the corners of his eyes creasing. Satisfaction looked good on his face. "Impressive quilt."

"Seriously, you should get one." I strained across his chest to retrieve an ashtray, lighter, and joint from the bedside table. I had rolled the joint earlier that morning, with this specific scene in mind.

He raised an eyebrow and folded an arm behind his head. "You got me drunk and seduced me, and now you're trying to get me high?"

"No pressure." I wadded a pillow behind my head and lit the joint. "And let's be real; you didn't even finish your first drink. I got myself drunk."

"True." He took the joint off my hands as soon as it was burning. "You did seduce me, though." He took two hits before passing it back.

I smoked and let my thoughts wander. They traveled to the party at my house, now Nicole's house. "Seeing you smoking with Kristin," I said, "that drove me crazy."

"I was thinking about that, too. I almost never smoke. You're a bad influence."

"Why did you let her kiss you?"

He fanned his fingers through the cloud hanging over us. "I don't know. It didn't mean anything. Being around you was difficult, so I went off with her."

"It was weird, when she was kissing you . . . I got mad . . . but I think I got kind of turned on." I passed the joint.

"I was trying not to think about you. When you came out on the deck"—he went silent briefly, holding a hit—"I saw you looking at me, I thought about your mouth on my neck. That was a problem. Yeah." He chuckled and closed his eyes. "Michael . . . when you moved out of your house, I thought about offering my place. Doesn't work, though. You know, my sister . . . she likes to surprise me."

"Oh, right." Maybe it was the smoke, but Cal's confession stunned me. He had considered allowing me to live with him? "Damn."

"My family, they can never know. They would . . . what is it Amish people do? Exile? Shun? Shun me."

"For real?"

"Yes, really. I was going to get you an apartment near me. That was my next idea. But I knew you wouldn't accept it."

"Yeah. No." I exhaled a big hit. "Wow, though."

"You fucking lightweight." Cal laughed helplessly as he slid the joint from my fingers. "If you could hear yourself."

I had to concentrate to remember what I had been saying: Mostly generic, monosyllabic words. I laughed with him. "Sorry."

"No, it's . . . don't apologize. I'm pretty high, too." He leaned over and kissed my mouth. The joint ended up in the ashtray. I kissed him slowly, my hands in his hair.

"You would live with me? Because I look like Jamie?"

"Jamie is dead." He spoke across my lips.

"What happened?" I released him and he sank onto his back beside me.

"I got Coral pregnant. We got married. I was writing, publishing." The telling of the story was staccato, Cal's voice empty. "Jamie looked me up. I hadn't heard from him for years. Nine years. He was grown up."

"He just showed up?"

"No, no. He e-mailed. He was . . . in advertising. He had some artistic ambition. I guess life crushed that out of him." He draped an arm across his eyes. "He wanted to meet up. We did, for lunch. He was happy for me. Even about my marriage, my son."

"Was he married?"

"No. He was single. We acted like nothing had happened. We didn't talk about that stuff. It upset me. We weren't like that before. We talked about everything before. I went home . . . got drunk, called him. I was angry. Turns out, so was he. Angry at me for moving on. I hadn't, though. I loved him."

Cal re-lit the joint and dragged on it deeply.

"We started up again. It was all right there. He worked in Baltimore . . . he would drive down. Hotels." He gestured. "I hated that. The hotels. So he got an apartment in Virginia. I told Coral everything short of the truth—that he was a Christian, that we'd been best friends. I said he commuted for work, like he worked in Virginia sometimes. We started building a car. It was an excuse to be spending so many weekends together. With Coral, after a while, I couldn't do things anymore."

"What do you mean?" I laid my cheek on the pillow and watched his profile. He looked dead. If he had closed his eyes, it would have frightened me.

"I couldn't perform. With her. I went to the doctor, to make it seem real. It was humiliating." The joint hissed. "Anyway, she wasn't stupid. She got suspicious and hired a PI. She confronted me with it . . . pictures, really graphic pictures. She wanted a divorce. She threatened to show my family, his family." He shook a hand through his hair. He had turned slightly yellow, like he was going to be sick.

"Do you need anything?"

"Water, I think."

I launched out of bed, dressed halfway, and brought him a cold bottle of water. He didn't thank me or even look at me, but he drank the whole bottle.

We sat on the edge of the bed, not quite side by side.

"Jamie . . . our families were the same. And we loved our families. But . . . Coral wanted full custody. How could I agree to that?" He gazed at the floor. "Jamie didn't want us to stop. He said his family couldn't know. I told him both of those things had to happen, because of my son, to have my son in my life. He went back to Baltimore and hung himself. In his closet. Nobody knew for a while. He lived alone, so."

I lowered my head. "Cal—"

"No. Don't say sorry to me. If I had left him alone in the first place, it would never have happened. And if I hadn't cheated on my wife. When she found out, that was all she needed. She wanted full custody, she wanted me to stop publishing, or she would tell his parents and brothers why he'd killed himself. How it was my fault. My part in it.

"We would have gone to court. She made a good point. She said I had ruined her life, so she ruined mine." He looked at me. "I hate that he had to be alone. He had to do it alone. Then he was hanging there by himself for so many days."

I felt sick to my stomach, but it was Cal who excused himself, turned into the bathroom, and vomited.

40

CALEB

WHEN I FINISHED TALKING ABOUT Jamie, I wanted to go home, but I was too fucked up to drive. Even after I vomited, I was staggeringly high.

Michael gave me a spare toothbrush and I cleaned myself up, splashed water on my face, and tied back my hair.

To vividly recall the past is to go there. To imagine the unspeakable—Jamie hanging in his closet for over a week—is to be there. I hadn't wanted to infect Michael's mind with those images. Only I deserved that.

We sat on his tiny deck and I smoked.

"I'm sorry," I said. "I was way off base with that."

"Huh?" He looked at me inattentively.

"Telling you that. It wasn't the time."

He sucked on a bottle of water. "I asked."

"You didn't know what you were asking." I put a hand on his shoulder. "I knew. I should have told you another time."

"Oh."

He may not have understood what I meant—we'd had sex for the first time and I had obliterated the occasion with my personal horror story—or he may not have cared.

"Let's go in," I said. "It's cold."

I poured myself a drink and he sat on the couch and stared at me. He had never looked so young, with his hair disheveled and his eyes glazed.

"You don't see your son?" he said.

"Once each summer, if that. We get together at my parents' place in Martha's Vineyard. They were furious with me, over the divorce. People don't divorce in my family. But she hasn't told them. She's kept up her end of the deal."

"Everyone thinks you let her have full custody without a fight?"

"Yeah. I told my parents she wanted it, and that I didn't want to go to court. I said she and I would work out our own arrangements."

"And you stopped publishing."

"Right."

"You let her do that to you?"

"I did it to myself, Michael."

"What do you even get out of this?" He was too high to be acting; he was legitimately dumbfounded. "Your family still talks to you? Jamie's family doesn't know they drove him to suicide by being bigots? How is that worth anything?"

"Don't." I gave him a warning look.

A small, flabbergasted laugh escaped him. "See? That look . . . I would swear you don't take bullshit from anyone, but this is so much bullshit."

Michael didn't understand, which was no surprise to me. In the lives of people without moral compasses, there is no value, no cost and worth. If Jamie had died and I had returned to my glowing literary career and a good relationship with my son, then there would have been no price for the mistakes I had made, no worth to his death, no cost to me. And Coral had deserved her vision of happiness: A faithful husband at her side, our son secure in a stable and healthy home. She deserved her justice.

"Let's agree to disagree," I said evenly.

Again, a hysterical laugh bubbled out of him. "I don't know. I guess."

Instead of trying to sober up, I drank more. We took a walk, watched a movie, and he showed me his stream setup. After four years, I had learned how to compartmentalize the past, more or less. For Michael, though, the story was too raw to ignore. He kept making brief, baffled comments—"I can't believe you never see your son" and "I can't believe his parents don't know why he died"—until I said, "Leave it alone," which he did.

Still, I disliked the subtle change in the way he looked at me, like he pitied me or doubted me somehow. And I hated his assessment of the situation—of me. *I would swear you don't take bullshit from anyone, but this is so much bullshit.*

The evening bled like watercolor, too much bourbon, and we got into Michael's cheap vodka afterward. I watched him play a computer game. It charmed me, his bulky headset and animated explanations, and I wanted to take him to bed, but neither of our moods had lifted enough for that.

Around ten, he said, "You should spend the night. You can't drive home."

"If you don't mind," I replied, which is about the last thing I remember.

41

CALEB

I WOKE TO A SENSATION I should not have been feeling: A hand on my inner thigh, a little stitch of pain as someone brushed a finger over a scabbing cut. My head pulsed and my breath scraped up my throat.

"Are you fucking kidding me?" Michael said.

Thin, rough sheets tangled over my naked body. I sat up swiftly and dragged them across my legs. Too late. Michael knelt on the bed, staring at my lap.

The room reeled and I clutched my forehead.

"Cal, what the hell?" His voice quavered pitifully. "What are those?"

By that point in time, I had half a dozen grinning gashes on either inner thigh, some almost healed, others crusted with dried blood. And my hung-over brain couldn't come up with one reasonable lie to explain them.

"Don't make a big thing of it." My voice was hoarse.

"Are you serious?"

"When did I undress?" I blinked against the morning light.

"We undressed last night. You don't remember."

"Obviously not." I swung my legs out of bed, carefully keeping the sheets in place. Michael had seen quite enough for one morning. "Did we—"

"We kissed and passed out."

"Good." Under his scrutiny, I tugged on my boxer briefs. He must have been pretty far gone, too, if he hadn't noticed the cuts last night.

He took a few steps, scratched his scalp, and shook his head. "Anemia."

"It's not a big deal."

"You've been doing that?"

"Relax, okay? It helps me. It's fine." I pulled on the rest of my clothes, which were strewn around the room. I hadn't gotten blackout drunk in years. I remembered the sex, the joint, talking about Jamie, sitting in Michael's office chair . . . and maybe I had tried to play one of his games. Yeah. We had laughed at my ineptitude.

He was silent, rubbing his face.

"Hey." I ran my knuckles down his spine.

"Dude, don't." He moved away.

Already, I could tell this was going to be worse than I had imagined.

"When I'm there?" He turned. "When you shower?"

"Not every time." That was true, but I could tell he didn't believe me.

"Do you know there's a fucking artery there?"

"I'm careful."

His face contorted. Many things must have made sense to him now: The black jeans, the fact that I never fully undressed, the bouts of dizziness and extreme pallor.

He wandered into the kitchen. He wouldn't look at me.

"It helps you," he deadpanned. "How?"

"Sometimes, I don't want to feel . . . desire, like that. Sometimes I actually want to resist. It helps calm me down."

"You want to resist feeling turned on. Because you think it's wrong." He made no effort to conceal his contempt.

"Don't use this to step on my beliefs."

"Your *beliefs* . . . are so fucked up. Everything about your life right now is so fucked up. I can't believe you were letting me do stuff with you and then going in your bathroom and cutting yourself because of it."

"I'm going to go." I shrugged on my coat.

"Yeah, please do." He nodded a few times, but then he swerved between the doorway and me. His face was blanched, his eyes reddish. "No."

"What is it?" I frowned down at him.

"Are you gonna . . ."

"No, Michael. It's not like that."

He was visibly afraid, which made me feel like a freak.

"I am not going to do it," I said firmly. "I'm fine. The few times I have, it was under control. You're blowing this out of proportion."

"I saw scars. Old scars."

"It's an on-again, off-again thing."

He sucked his bottom lip between his teeth and sighed out through his nose. "So, it's on-again because of me."

Now I was afraid, because this conversation only ended with Michael leaving me in a misguided effort to help me.

"I'm hungry. I'm hung over. I'm going home." I moved around him. "Calm down about this. I'll see you on Monday."

My chest froze up when, halfway to my car, I heard sneakers pelting behind me.

I turned and saw Michael, haphazardly dressed, keys in hand.

"I'll follow you up," he said.

Between relief and frustration, I didn't know where to land.

"Whatever you want." I slammed my car door.

42

MICHAEL

Maybe the best thing I could have done that day was get some distance and time away from Cal. Like a powerful narcotic, he warped my reality. He told me that insane lines of thought were aspects of his faith and that pathological behaviors were *fine, helpful, no big deal*. And when he said those things so calmly and looked at me with his handsome, composed face, out of his life of wealth and privilege, I almost believed him.

But I was afraid to leave him alone. And I loved him. Too late, I had witnessed the disturbing history around him and been invited into his twisted psyche. Maybe, if he had told me about Jamie and his wife early on, or if I had seen the self-inflicted gouges on his thighs, I would have walked away out of a sense of self-preservation. Maybe.

But probably not.

Love is a cage two people build around themselves. Cal and Jamie had locked themselves in that cage and it had cost them everything. Now I was trapped with Cal, trailing his Audi to Red Feather, unable and unwilling to escape.

The first serious snow had fallen on his property. There had been other, smaller snowfalls, which gathered like foam and blew away or melted in hours, but this one was heavy, deep, and silencing. It seemed fitting.

My Jeep slid and skidded up the hill and Cal, ahead of me, slowed until we reached his house. We walked inside together, as if things were normal.

"I'm going to shovel the walk," he said.

Under different circumstances, I would have joked about my first catastrophic appearance on his walkway. As was, I hovered while he retrieved a shovel from the garage. I felt useless and slightly ridiculous, but also stubbornly determined.

"I'll help."

"You're not dressed for it. It won't take me a moment."

I might have argued that he wasn't dressed for the twenty-degree morning, either, but his front closet was packed with thermal jackets, boots, gloves, hats, and scarves. He shrugged on a black North Face jacket before going out.

I stood on the stoop, snow soaking into my Vans, and watched him. It took him a moment to notice me.

"Michael."

"I'm fine." I controlled my chattering teeth. "It feels nice out here."

"Go inside."

"Seriously, I want to be out here."

Hair straggled across his face in the icy wind. He shoved it back and glared at me.

"Go inside, put on boots and a real jacket."

With that offer, I relented, dashing inside to exchange my puffy coat for a thick Patagonia jacket and my canvas sneakers for heavy, fur-lined boots. I also snagged another shovel from the garage. He smirked at me when I reappeared. It was a fond smirk, not a cruel one, and it chipped at my anger and fear.

"What?" I mumbled.

"You're all ready to build a snowman."

"Ha, ha."

"No?" He approached. "Going to make a snow angel?"

I tried to ignore him, driving my shovel into the snow, but he caught my collar and brought my face close to his. His breath was warm and sweet on my face. "Make a snow angel, Michael," he whispered, brushing his lips over mine. "It would be so fitting."

It took all my willpower to push him away.

"I'm really not in the mood, man."

He chuckled and resumed shoveling. "Suit yourself."

We made quick work of the walkway and deck. The dry cold and my hangover parched my throat. We guzzled water in the kitchen. Next, he headed for the loft.

"What now?" I followed anxiously.

"Gonna work out. I drank too much last night. Gotta get it out of my system."

He said nothing, though he smiled thinly, when I pursued him upstairs. I loitered by the closet as he changed into a pair of sweats. Then we went down to the basement, me floating after him like a bee, where he kept his bench and weights, a rowing machine, and a treadmill. He turned on music. I didn't recognize the song. It was sad, mostly in the minor key, but with a driving, hypnotic rhythm.

"You're welcome to run or whatever," he said, strapping on lifting gloves and lying back on the bench, "though I think there's a . . . wardrobe hurdle, again."

Fleetingly, I pictured myself hitting the treadmill in boxers. I wanted to laugh, but I didn't let myself. Things were not okay. He needed to know that.

"I'm good, thanks." I opened my laptop on the carpet and sat against the wall, and I tried my best to ignore him as he did reps with loaded bars. Getting turned on wouldn't help anything today. I glanced at his arms and shoulders, the veins standing out, sweat shining on his skin. I opened a webpage titled *How to Support Someone Who Self-Harms*.

He was breathing hard. The noise was impossible to block out.

He had breathed that way during sex, like it was killing him.

And maybe it was killing him.

The webpage waxed on about patience and compassion. I navigated back and clicked another hit. Somehow, the second page was worse. It told me not to judge him and not to tell him to stop. It said I shouldn't ask to see his injuries. *Bullshit.*

After twenty or so minutes, Cal moved to the pull-up bar. I let myself take one look at his back.

Yet another site suggested alternatives to self-harm: Snapping a rubber band against one's wrist, squeezing ice, drawing with a red pen instead of cutting, writing down feelings and tearing up the paper. I gritted my teeth. Were these people for real?

I could have laughed or cried. *Try creative outlets like singing, dancing, or writing poetry to express the emotions that make you want to self-harm.* Oh, yes, why hadn't I thought of that? Cal could do interpretive dance instead of slicing up his legs.

"You doing okay?"

I jumped and shut my laptop. He stood in front of me, sweat-soaked and carved with lean muscle. I looked away.

"Fine, do your thing."

"I'm nearly done." He crouched and rubbed my ankle. "You sure you're okay?"

"Yeah, really." My voice caught. I tucked my foot away from his fingers.

He grinned like the devil and moved off to do sets of sit-ups and pushups.

When he finally finished and headed upstairs to shower, I stuck to his heels.

"How is this going to work?" he said, standing in the bathroom.

By way of an answer, I sat on top of the toilet and opened my laptop.

What I had really wanted the Internet to tell me was that I, as a sane and well-adjusted human, had the right—the obligation, even—to drag Cal to the nearest psychiatrist, who would confirm that he was sick and needed help.

"You could join me." He combed a hand through my hair.

"Where do you keep the knife?" I studied my knees. I knew damn well that the knife was in the bottom drawer on the right, since I had searched his bathroom once.

He took it out and handed it to me. "Happy?"

"Oh, yeah." I shook my head, closing my hand around the sturdy little weapon. "I'm really happy, Cal."

"Don't make it like this." He stroked the side of my neck. "Undress me. Shower with me." His voice dropped. "I'll put it in your mouth."

I had to shut my eyes. How could he invite me like that, when he found our intimacy so repulsive that he might end up hurting himself to *resist* it?

"You're an asshole," I said. "Don't be in there too long."

43

MICHAEL

Cal took a five-minute shower, toweled off behind the curtain, and headed for his closet. I had rebuffed him at least three times and he finally seemed miffed. He dressed in off-white lounge pants and a Henley shirt and jogged downstairs as if I weren't there.

The pale pants, I knew, were for my sake. *Look, Michael: No blood.*

For the time being, I tucked his knife into my laptop case. I wanted to throw it away, but it was a Benchmade, meaning it cost over a hundred dollars, and anyway, if Cal really wanted to hurt himself, there were dozens of knives in the kitchen. I couldn't throw them all away. I couldn't replace his utensils with plastic spoons. I couldn't follow him around for the rest of his life.

I drifted glumly into the family room and sat on the couch.

He was at the stove, cooking something. Every slide and ting of silverware made me flinch. Should I have showered with him?

Was he more or less likely to hurt himself now? Was he five seconds away from plunging a cooking knife into his stomach?

The tension grated along my nerves until my whole body was singing with fear.

"Michael."

I peered over at him. He had set two plates at the kitchen table.

"Breakfast," he said.

"Oh." And now I felt like a douchebag. I wandered over and sat in front of an omelet and a glass of orange juice.

"I hope you like spinach."

I gave him a leery glance. "Spinach is fine."

He sat beside me, prayed, and cut into his omelet. Leaves of spinach and cheese stretched between thin layers of egg.

"I'm fine," he said. He could actually read my thoughts. "I just like spinach."

"That time you passed out . . ."

"I was tired. I fell asleep."

"No, you passed out." I stared at my omelet, my mouth souring. "You could have died. I wouldn't have known. Or you could have needed medical attention, and I would have been sitting there like an idiot when I should have been calling for help."

"What exactly do you want?" He lowered his fork.

I wanted him to stop. I wanted him to be free. I wanted to change the way he saw himself and the world. "I want"—I cleared my throat—"to spend the night."

"Will that make you feel better?"

I nodded, because technically it would make me feel better, for the night.

"Fine. Knock yourself out." He continued eating.

"Could I show you something?"

He didn't look up from his food. "Sure."

I retrieved a rubber band from my laptop case. I couldn't believe I was actually doing this. (That quote about desperate times is appropriate here.)

"I read this online." I took his hand and stretched the rubber band around his wrist. "So, when you want to . . ." His dark eyes bored into me. I nearly lost my nerve. "Well, it's a coping technique." Gently, I snapped the rubber band against his wrist.

He continued to stare at me for a while and I wondered if he was going to laugh in my face or order me to leave. He did neither. Instead, he brushed a thumb over my cheek and smiled sadly. "I see. Thank you."

As always, his off-kilter response flustered me. "Yeah, no problem. There were other things. I mean, some of them were stupid, but . . ."

"But this one was a keeper."

The dry humor in his voice hit me wrong. I stuffed a bite of omelet into my mouth and swallowed past the lump in my throat. At least I was trying.

"That was a joke," he said.

"It's not funny."

"You won't let me hold you. You won't let me show you affection." He pushed away his plate. "I don't know how else to comfort you."

"You think showing me affection is wrong. Do you get why I can't let you do it if you feel that way?"

"Honestly? No." He sounded sincerely nonplussed. "I know it's wrong, but that's between me and God. It's not your problem."

"It is if you . . ." My hands shook. Why was this so difficult to talk about? "If you do that to yourself. That makes it my problem."

He stayed quiet.

"Have you ever considered the possibility that it's not wrong? What if your family and your religion are wrong about this?"

His silence was becoming ominous.

"I'm not trying to be rude," I continued, "but Christianity is—"

"My turn to show you something." He excused himself, went to the office, and returned with a manuscript box. He pushed it toward me. "Go on."

My pulse quickened as I lifted the lid.

A slab of papers lay in the box and the top page read *The House of Faith by Caleb Bright*, which wasn't the title of any of his other books. "Is this—"

"My fourth novel," he said. "I stopped publishing. I didn't stop writing."

I flipped through the front matter. "Can I?"

"Go for it." He shook a cigarette from his pack. "You can write about it in your profile. How's that?"

"Are you serious?"

"Yeah. Talk about it all you want"—he gestured to the manuscript—"so long as it's clear I won't be publishing it. That'll drive people crazy."

"Cal, this . . ." I shook my head. "This is huge."

"I know." He took his plate to the sink. "You deserve it."

44

CALEB

MICHAEL SPENT THE REST OF the day in an armchair near the fireplace, reading my book. I felt obligated to stay close, because whenever I ventured out of the room, he looked after me with wide, troubled eyes. He seemed to think I was on the verge of suicide. Sharp noises made him jump. More than once, tears of frustration brimmed in his eyes.

He was a foreign creature to me, both in his easy emotionality and simple acceptance of our intimacy. For me, it was torture—to want his male body, to feel desire stirring in mine—like a slow, painful, undefeatable cancer.

Meanwhile, he was as free as a child, unhindered by any knowledge of morality, a true innocent in the garden.

I envied him, and his carefree ignorance made me want him more, as if I could somehow draw his happiness into myself.

Mindlessly, I snapped the rubber band against my wrist.

I had situated myself on the couch with a book, though I spent most of my time rebuilding the fire and watching Michael read. The flames gave his skin a soft orange cast. His hair swept low across his brow, almost into his eyes. He had thick, dark lashes and the color of his iris was a pure, golden brown, like wheat.

His eyes flickered up from the page. They were far away, lost in my story.

"Oh," he said, shifting in the chair. "You're sure you don't mind if I just read?"

"Read away. That's all I do, some days." I tapped the neglected book on my lap.

"This is really good."

"Thanks." I smiled and stretched along the couch. His gaze responded, skipping over the length of my body. He looked away abruptly.

"Doesn't it make you angry?"

"What?"

"Writing something this good"—he motioned with the manuscript—"putting so much work into something, and not being able to share it."

"Oh." I closed my eyes and snapped the rubber band. His words drifted, feather light, across my mind. I liked the sound of his voice and the way his throat hummed when he spoke, when I had my lips on it. I liked his reluctant pauses and silly T-shirts. I liked his impractical, flimsy sneakers and his boyish boxers.

Anger. He wanted to know about anger.

My thoughts ticked toward Coral and I drew back the rubber band, hard, and it stung my skin. Wasn't it enough, in the way of revenge, for her to have cost me the only person I had ever truly loved? Did she also need to take my son, my career?

I imagined my hands around her neck, her face turning gray.

Nobody knows as much about anger as I do.

"You think it's easy for me," I said. "This arrangement."

"I don't know. You seem pretty accepting."

I smirked. What Michael viewed as acceptance, I viewed as dignity. I was simply not pissing my pants on the executioner's block.

"I mean, you said you did it to yourself. Like you really think you deserve this." He wasn't trying to argue with me. His voice came from a place of pain and confusion. He was trying to reason with me.

"I do believe I deserve it," I admitted. "That doesn't make it any easier." Before he could continue, I rose and stretched. Again, he gave me a nearly involuntary lookover. "I'd like to sketch you, if you don't mind. You can stay right there."

"Oh." He smoothed his hair. "Sure, I guess. That makes me kind of nervous."

"That's not much of a change for you, is it?" I grinned and headed to the annex.

45

CALEB

That evening, I sketched Michael until the sunlight withdrew from the room and we had to turn on lamps to supplement the fire. I filled page after page with the sprawl of his legs, the incline of his head, his inattentive features and easy posture. One page, I devoted entirely to his hands, which were miraculously still as he read.

I have always preferred drawing to photography, because photos only reveal what is, but the sketch reveals what is felt. And that's art—the irrepressible filter of feeling between the self and the world. As I interpreted Michael into graphite lines, I focused on affection instead of shame, and on the growing love I felt for him instead of the hatred I felt for myself. Of course, I was falling in love with him. He had witnessed all of my darkness and he was still at my side.

"Can I see?" he asked, not for the first time. We had spent the whole day on reading and drawing, breaking only for lunch, dinner, and cigarettes.

I walked over and inclined the sketchbook.

He studied the page seriously.

"You're good at everything."

"You don't really believe that," I replied. About the things that mattered—love and intimacy, a healthy and fair-minded view of the world and myself—he believed I failed completely. I watched him process my comment and close his mouth.

"I'm tired, Michael. I'm heading up."

"Oh." He hopped out of the chair. "Me too."

"You could stay down here, make yourself at home."

"No, I'm tired." Contrary to the statement, his face was pale and alert.

"Well, there's a guest room in the basement." I put out the fire and closed curtains and blinds. I knew he wanted to babysit me and it might have been amusing to watch him squirm if I didn't offer my bed, but he had been through enough in the last twenty-four hours. "Or you can sleep with me."

"Sure," he mumbled.

I gave him a toothbrush and kicked him out of the bathroom for a few minutes of privacy. He was waiting by the door when I emerged.

"You're welcome to do a full body exam," I said, stripping lazily as I crossed the room. "Or maybe some forensic work in there."

"Very funny." He darted into the bathroom.

It *was* funny to me, his mounting uneasiness over our sleeping arrangement. I tossed my clothes in the hamper, turned off the lights, and stretched out, naked, beneath the sheets. I rarely slept naked, but Michael didn't need to know that.

His shadowy shape appeared in the bathroom doorway, boxer-clad, carrying a pile of folded clothes. "I'll just . . ."

"Put them anywhere," I murmured.

"Okay." He shuffled cautiously toward the bed.

"Watch your step." I grinned in the dark.

"You're a dick." The comforter shifted and he scooted onto the mattress with minimal movement. And there he stayed, tightly curled at the far side of the bed. I yawned and stretched and waited.

"I think I need to invest in sheets with a higher thread count," he said.

"Hm," I agreed.

"Thanks for letting me stay."

I made another affable noise.

He was actually going to say goodnight, as if we were boys at a sleepover. I could feel it coming. I steeled myself.

"Anyway"—he cleared his throat—"goodnight, Cal."

My shoulders trembled and my throat clamped powerlessly around my laughter, so that it came out gravelly and suppressed.

"What?" he said. "What is it?"

"Come here, Michael."

He inched over until his spine touched my flank.

I rolled onto my side and pulled his back against my chest, nestling my erection into the cleft of his bottom. Only then did he realize I was naked and he jumped. I touched his chest, brushing my fingers over his nipples. They were terrifically sensitive. I teased them for a while, making him twitch against me.

"Cal..."

"What?" I felt him through his boxers. He was rigid.

"I don't... want you to get turned on and... hurt yourself."

"It's a little late, for the first part. And I won't, okay?" I pressed against him. "I won't." I needed him so badly, I would have agreed to anything.

"You have to finish," he said.

"I will. I promise. You can watch." I pushed down his boxers and he twisted to face me. We touched each other gently, kissing and rubbing together. When he dragged back the covers and moved down my body, I let him go, my fingers woven into his hair as he kissed my shaft. He had no idea what he was doing and, somehow, his inexperience was incredibly arousing. I moaned sharply as he sucked on my head.

"Michael . . . use your hands."

He obeyed at once, clumsily squeezing my balls and shaft. I would have been laughing, if I weren't gasping and writhing. In my limited experience, growing up with a male body never quite prepares one for handling the same.

He tried to take me deep and gagged, backing off and panting. As he collected himself, he kissed my abs, then my thighs, then my inner thighs, his lips and tongue caressing my cuts and scars. Teardrops hit my skin.

I pulled him up and kissed the damp tracks from his cheeks. Then I kissed his mouth, sliding my tongue in and out suggestively.

When I reached for my lubricant, he started to roll over.

"No," I said, positioning him on his back. "Like this."

I lifted his legs over my shoulders and penetrated him. I told him I could get deeper that way, and that I knew he wanted to keep an eye on me. I made him touch himself and I watched as I rocked into him. He came first, always.

I enjoyed him for a long time afterward, slamming against him, slowing down, riding the edge of ecstasy and telling him every filthy thought that crossed my mind.

While we did it, I made him look at me, and we kissed and I touched him. I never wanted to stop. He was perfect, trapped between discomfort and pleasure, and when I rode him hard, he gripped the sheets and made the most obscene noises.

Sweat dripped from my chin to his chest. "Good," he said continually, "it feels good," even though he winced when I went too fast. "Doesn't it feel good?" he panted, pulling my body against his.

I nodded, slowly losing my grip on control.

"Because it *is* good," he said. "It's good, Cal. It's okay."

He drew my lips to his as I came and he kissed me as if he could change my mind with a kiss. I moaned into his mouth. He clutched at me then and after, his limbs like bars around me, and when I woke the next morning he was still clinging to me.

46

MICHAEL

Cal made love to me again in the morning. I was sore and it hurt, but I liked what it did to him, and I even liked the pain. I froze each time he slid his deepest or moved too roughly, but the proof of my pleasure hung between my legs, stiff and dripping.

And it was different from the first time. He made it last. He kissed me and embraced me and talked to me, and we moved together.

Afterward, though, a familiar dread swamped me as he headed to the bathroom.

"Are you going to shower?" I jogged after him.

"I usually do, in the morning."

"I thought you worked out first."

"I think I got my heart rate up enough last night." He smirked over his shoulder. "And this morning. Something on your mind?"

He was naked and morning light streamed into the room, tingeing his hair blue. He seemed unnaturally comfortable in his skin, whereas I had tugged on my boxers moments after sex. There were no visible wounds on the back of his body, no faded scars. If he turned around, I would have been able to see the gashes on his inner thighs, and I did want to see them clearly. The morning I had discovered them was a hazy, hung-over memory, and I had barely looked at them before he had woken up.

He watched me as I inspected his body and he chuckled. "Don't tell me you're ready for round two. I know you're younger than I am, but that would be impressive."

"Oh, no." My gaze snapped up. "Maybe I'll shower, too."

"Good. It's awkward when you sit on the toilet. Makes me feel like a specimen."

I tried to detect any disappointment in his expression or voice, but he seemed genuinely pleased. In the shower, we kissed and he held me against the tiles. Then he shampooed his hair and mine and washed our bodies. That was heaven—an unexpected pleasure—the feeling of his long, powerful hands massaging my skull and limbs. I groaned and rolled back my head. His teeth closed gently on my throat.

It came naturally to me, to let him take control in so many ways. I could never have imagined our roles in reverse. And I considered myself strong and strong-willed, opinionated, intelligent, and self-motivated. Maybe, once, I had needed Nicole to bump my life in a productive direction, but my relationship with Cal bore no trace of that. I felt no pressure from him to be or do something more than I was. If anything, he exerted a kind of passive influence, making me want to be the best possible version of myself. I wondered what he would have thought of me three years ago.

His finger slid into my backside and he closed his eyes and kissed my ear. "Can't help myself," he whispered.

"Cal." I gripped his hair.

"I want to see if I can . . ." He fingered me slowly. I knew what he wanted to do—he wanted to see if he could bring me to climax again—and he did, easily, on his knees with his mouth around me and his finger still moving inside of me.

I stepped out of the shower, dazed. He toweled off my hair, a small grin on his lips. "Impressive," he murmured.

Unthinkingly, my gaze fell to his soft member, and then to the cuts on his thighs. They were like shark gills, arranged in neat rows, six per leg. Three were an angry brownish-red; four were slim and pink; the rest were pale, vanishing.

"Take a picture," he said.

I continued to study them. His subtle sarcasm didn't bother me. I was, truly enough, trying to take a mental picture so that I would know if he did it again.

"I'm just looking," I said. "Do you mind?"

"I guess not." He dried his hair and arms.

The websites I had visited yesterday had cautioned against this—*don't focus on the wounds or ask to see them*—and against making ultimatums, which seemed ridiculous to me. If Cal kept slicing into his leg because of us, I would have to leave him, or at least threaten to leave him. My chest constricted at the thought.

"I'm not going to do it," he said calmly, wrapping the towel around his waist and ending my examination. "You don't have to worry."

"Is it that easy to stop?"

"I didn't say it was easy. I said I'm not going to do it." He walked to his closet. I followed, yanking on my jeans. I couldn't wear my boxers again, they were a mess, and I felt grungy putting on yesterday's rumpled clothes. I needed to go home. My stomach turned to lead, sinking inside of me.

"You're stopping for me?"

"I don't want to make you unhappy. Anyway, you wouldn't put up with that, would you?" He asked the question in an offhanded tone, but I could tell by the set of his shoulders, and by the tension in his arms as he pulled up his jeans, that he didn't feel half as relaxed as he sounded.

You wouldn't put up with that, would you?
You would leave me, wouldn't you?
"That's . . . I don't know."

"It's fine," he said, browsing through his shirts. "I think I'd feel the same way, in your position. You can't stay with someone who's doing that, right? Especially not if it's a result of your being together." He chose a gray long-sleeved shirt. He paused before taking it off the hanger. "If you were doing that to yourself, I would go crazy."

He understood, then. I exhaled. "I feel like I am, honestly."

"Well, I don't want that." He moved back to the bathroom. "I wouldn't be able to leave you, though. Even if you couldn't stop. It's past that, now. For me." He tousled product into his hair and brushed his teeth. I brushed mine, too, my eyes lowered.

It was easy for him to say he couldn't leave me. I wanted to tell him it was the same for me, but that information might be dangerous in his hands. If he could hurt himself and keep me, he might go back to it. Then I would have to weigh those two incredible pains: The pain of staying with him while he was hurting himself and the pain of never seeing him again. I stared into the bowl of the sink, my stomach cramping. Never in my life had emotional turmoil taken such a toll on my body.

"Anyway," he said, "I don't have much of a choice. I hate to put this on you, but I can't lose you. So, I won't do it anymore. Try not to worry."

He kissed my shoulder and headed downstairs.

He had as good as told me he loved me—*I can't lose you*—and I stood there for a while processing the information, letting it wash against me like a tide. I thought it couldn't be true, yet everything in my reality told me it was. I was the object of his physical and emotional desire. His fascinating mind, his complicated heart, and his incredible body were all, somehow, fixated on me, and he couldn't lose me.

47

MICHAEL

I TRIED TO READ MORE of Cal's novel, but my day-old clothes smelled stale, I hated feeling scruff every time I leaned on my hand, and, as the hours passed, I began to realize how silly it was to try to stay at his house indefinitely. I had to go home, if only for a change of clothes and a stick of deodorant.

I fit his manuscript carefully into the box and closed my laptop. I had begun taking notes on the book and even nailed a real first line for the profile: *Caleb Bright's fourth novel is a mesmerizing psychological portrait of a family shaped and shattered by faith, but you'll probably never read it.*

"Had enough?" he said. Sometimes, he seemed absorbed in his sketching or reading, yet he never missed my smallest motion.

"Oh, no way. It's incredible, Cal." I meant that. I had enjoyed his first three books, but I had force-fed them to myself in less than a week, which is much too fast for a slow reader. *The House of Faith*, though, made his earlier work look like practice—like he had finally taken off his training wheels and flown.

The novel's heroine was orbiting further and further from her family's conventions and, consequently, from that harbor of love and identity. Soon, I sensed, she would try to make her way back and find the path blocked. It was a prodigal daughter story, but without forgiveness, and I read much of Cal's struggle into it.

"You think so?"

"Yeah. I think it's your best." I gripped the manuscript box and stared at the lid. "It's more personal than the others, if that makes sense."

"Sure it does."

"I see a lot of you in the protagonist."

"Well, that always happens." He closed his book and I could tell he wanted to close that conversation, too. "You can hang on to that copy, by the way. I have more."

"Oh. Thank you." I tucked the box against my stomach. "You don't mind if I mark it up?" I had been itching to dog-ear pages, highlight, and take margin notes.

"Not at all. It's yours."

"Thanks. Seriously." I smiled faintly. My stomach was churning.

"You're welcome." His lips twitched. "Seriously."

"I feel really grungy." I scratched my prickly jaw. "I need to shave and get clean clothes and stuff."

"That makes sense."

I remained seated, gazing at my socks. "I don't really want to go."

"I can see that." He wasn't helping me at all.

"You're probably ready to get rid of me." I forced a laugh.

"No." He folded his hands and watched me calmly.

"Oh. Well, maybe I'll just . . . run home and get clean clothes, then."

"Whatever you want, Michael."

"I could come back."

"I would like that."

Still, I was glued to the armchair. The thought of leaving him alone, with God knew how many sharp objects, was impossible. I pictured him unconscious in the bathtub, blood pumping from his open leg, and my heart began to palpitate.

"Listen," I said. "You should come with me."

"To your place?"

"Yeah. I'm only gonna drive down and back. Company would be nice." I knew I wasn't fooling him, but my dignity demanded I try.

"If that would make you happy." He didn't need to smirk or grin to let me know that my fear was obvious. Maybe he even felt sorry for me.

"It would."

"Fair enough. How about I drive, though. My car does better in the snow."

"That's fine. If you don't mind." I stacked my things and headed for my shoes and coat. I wouldn't mind watching him drive—not at all—and anyway, the Jeep's rickety handling had embarrassed me when I had driven him down for the party.

He took the Audi. Soft instrumental music drifted from the speakers. He drove sensibly, his dark eyes flickering between mirrors and the road, and from time to time he glanced at me, at which point I would pretend to have been watching the scenery. His sly smile told me he was not deceived.

"Nice view, right?" he said.

I raised the collar of my coat. Cal never seemed to flush, but it was my curse. I had Danish blood on my mother's side and Irish on my father's and the luminously pale skin to prove it. In cold weather, my cheeks got rosy like a girl's. Anger, embarrassment, and passion never failed to redden my face and neck, and sometimes, to my eternal shame, my eyes. In middle school, because my flushing was such a source of amusement to my peers, I had learned to recognize the subtle warmth and tingling that indicated I was making my transition to cooked lobster, so that I could hide or turn away until it passed. But there was no hiding or turning away from Cal, most of the time.

"Yeah, it's nice," I mumbled.

"You could have left that at my place." He meant the manuscript box, which was sitting on my lap.

"Oh. I didn't think of that."

"Could have left your laptop, too."

"Yeah, you're right. I wasn't sure . . ."

"I want you around, Michael. I told you—I would have moved you in, or closer, if not for my sister's habit of showing up unannounced. But she literally just did that, so we're safe for a couple months."

The way he phrased it—*safe*—made me feel his fear of exposure.

"Would your family really shun you, if they knew?"

"Oh, yes. Absolutely. I would not be invited to their homes, into their lives. It's a very big deal for us. And Coral's family is Southern Baptist. Extremely so."

I nodded slowly. To me, extreme Baptists were the people who had protested at the funerals of Orlando shooting victims. In other words, unfathomably small-minded individuals who took their faith to hateful extremes. I picked at the manuscript box and wondered if I was sitting beside a man like that. Cal didn't hurt or hate others, as far as I could tell, but he hurt and hated himself, and that was religious extremism, too.

"You understand now?" he said.

"I'm starting to."

"It's not what you're probably thinking. My family and hers, they're not hicks running around with assault weapons, trying to burn all the gays." He shook his head. "They're wealthy and well-educated. Cosmopolitan, even. But they're old families founded entirely on Christian faith. We know what we believe. We've believed it for generations. Atheists rely on the government to tell them what's right and wrong"—he waved a hand, dismissive—"which is so insane, if you think about it.

Sure, our current democracy has a humanitarian set of laws, but what happens if a government arises that says it's okay to kill under certain circumstances? Technically, you could say we already have that government, with late-term abortion being legal."

I watched him as he spoke. It was clear that he had considered this topic often and thoroughly. His thoughts were organized, his explanation patient.

He studied me for a moment. "Did you know that they strain away from the abortion tool, in the womb? Babies, I mean. Their heart rates increase, their motions become frantic, and their mouths open like they're crying or screaming. They actually move to try to escape the instrument. As if they could. And there's no one to help them."

I frowned and looked away. "I . . . no. I haven't really researched it."

"It's backwards and barbaric. The same things you think of my faith, I'm sure." His gaze returned to the road. "The truth is, morality means nothing in the hands of a secular government. Faith—God—gives us a set of rules with divine authority. And trust me, I wish I could change some of the rules, but it doesn't matter. It's not my choice. I'm glad it's not my choice. I'm not so confident that I'd feel comfortable deciding how everyone should live, or where we came from and where we're going. And it's obvious to me that humanity is too complicated and beautiful to be a fluke. Nothing about life makes sense outside of faith. Not to me, anyway."

I had no comeback, no response to his poised declaration. Sitting there beside me, he looked so sure of himself, and his argument made sense. When it came to right and wrong, I answered to American legislation. He answered to his God.

"I didn't mean to lecture you," he said after a while.

"No, you're fine. I want to know this stuff. I'm just thinking." And so I did—we had a long drive ahead of us—until I found a fault in his logic. "What about other faiths?" I said.

"There are so many. You talked about a government supporting murder, but some extreme faiths actually do. People blow up buildings, shoot up clubs. I know you'll say that's not okay, but they think it is. They don't want to answer to man-made laws, either. They think they're acting on behalf of a higher power."

"You're right. But that's not my faith, is it?"

"No," I persisted, "but it's *a* faith. I mean, there's obviously a problem with answering to higher powers however we see fit. We need laws."

"I don't disagree. The Bible advocates submitting to government rule."

"But you think one faith is right and the others are all wrong?"

He smirked. "I guess I do."

"So you're not comfortable making rules for everyone, but you've decided Christianity is the only real truth?"

He went quiet for a minute.

"You've got me there," he finally said.

I smiled a little. It was a small victory, but perhaps a large step toward helping him. And I wanted to help him. I was in this for as long as he would have me.

Without looking, he reached over and grazed his knuckles down my cheek. The gesture always made me want to nuzzle into his hand.

"Let me tell you something, though," he said, wrapping his fingers back around the wheel. "What I believe . . . I think you see it as something constructed around me."

"Kind of," I admitted. *Completely* was what I meant. Cal lived in his silver cage, though his heart had outgrown it years ago.

"Well, it's more like my bones, Michael. It's what I'm constructed around. Like Abigail." He gestured to the manuscript box. Abigail was the main character in *The House of Faith*. "If my faith broke apart somehow, so would I."

48

CALEB

At the apartment, Michael paced around the family room, repeated several times that he would "just grab a few things real fast," and then brought a set of folded clothes to the couch. I sat in the kitchen and watched.

"Oh, lemme shave." He disappeared again, returning smooth-faced and with a handful of toiletries. "For tomorrow morning," he explained. "If, I mean, if—"

"Good," I said. "It would be nice if you stayed over." I smiled pleasantly and spread my hands on the counter. I never quite knew what to do to put Michael at ease and my best efforts always seemed to backfire. Something about my very presence in his apartment made him jittery.

"Are you sure?"

"Absolutely. Stay over, please. If you want to."

"I do. If you want me to."

I gave him a dry look. He was becoming ridiculous, in a charming way.

"Get a bag for your toiletries," I said, because he had piled a bunch of products, loose, on a towel. "And a few more changes of clothes."

The stack on the couch grew until I had to advise him to get another bag.

The only suitable thing he owned was a small carry-on suitcase, which sent him into new conniptions.

"I can't believe this is all I have." He wheeled out the case, his face bright red. "I feel like I'm moving in. I swear, I used to own a gym bag."

"That's fine."

"I'll leave whenever you want. Is this too much?"

"No, it's perfect." I wanted to laugh, but that would have made matters worse. "Please, don't worry. I want you to stay."

"I'm an over-packer." He moved garments into the suitcase. "Not that I'm, like, taking a trip. I just want to stop stealing your toothpaste."

"Everything is fine. No problem." I prowled across the room, seeking a change of topic. I stopped in front of an odd decoration: A flattened balloon in a glass frame. Something indecipherable was scribbled on the balloon. "Modern art?"

"Oh." He laughed, the color on his neck deepening. "No, I . . . that was a joke with some work buddies. I used to work at Party World."

I grinned over my shoulder. "Party World?"

"Your party starts here," he mumbled.

"Don't I know it. Please tell me you wore one of the aprons."

He glowered at me. "You've actually set foot in a Party World?"

"More like I've walked past and glanced in the window." I chuckled. "When was this, and what's up with the balloon? Memento of happier times?"

"You're evil, dude." He zipped the suitcase. "We used to race, see who could prepare bunches of balloons fastest. I won.

That was my award slash going-away gift when I quit." He shrugged. "It was like four . . . three years ago."

"You seem so young to me." I moved behind him, sliding my hand into his hair.

"You wouldn't have looked at me twice, back then."

"Maybe we wouldn't have met," I said, "but if we had, I would have looked at you much more than twice." I brought my mouth close to the back of his neck. I wanted to kiss him there so much. Our conversation in the car, though, was still too close. I had told him what I believed, and what I believed condemned our relationship. If only I could have kept him near without giving in to physical desire. Then he would still have a girlfriend and a normal, decent life.

Instead, I had dragged him into my sin, and that was many times worse than keeping it to myself.

I drew back from him and made a fist.

I wanted to hurt myself, but, somehow, I was never supposed to do that again.

49

MICHAEL

Cal descended into a strange mood on the way back to Red Feather. He was quiet, but not inattentive, friendly, but not flirty or amused. He was half of himself and I couldn't decide if that owed to our conversation about his faith, the fact that I was practically moving in, or my status as a former Party World employee. I smiled slightly at my own joke. He didn't ask what was funny.

That night, he barely touched me. When I gathered the nerve to scoot against his side, he threw an arm over my back and went to sleep.

The next morning, though, he woke me with an almost painfully intense blowjob—the kind where he took me so deep that I wanted to scream. Then he tried to get out of bed without coming. I banded a leg around him and took hold of his shaft, one hand in his hair. "Let me," I pleaded.

He did just that. He closed his eyes, braced his arms against the mattress, and hovered over me as I jerked him off. He came with a tortured groan, like I had hurt him.

But, afterward, his mood evened out. We exercised and showered and he held me. I would have paid to know what was going through his head, but asking about it might have brought him back down, and his dark moods worried me.

On the porch, coffee and cigarette in hand, he said, "Sometimes I think these desires I have are like an addiction. If I didn't feed them, they might sort of fade."

I pretended the words didn't disturb me. "What would you want with me then? Ideally, I mean. If anything."

"Close companionship. Affection. Nothing intimate."

"I could try that, if it would help you. We could do that."

"Could you?" he said thoughtfully.

I nodded a little.

"Then you're stronger than I am"—he put out his cigarette, cupped the back of my neck, and kissed the top of my head—"because I can't."

Our days fell into a routine. We woke up and worked out, showered and ate breakfast, and read and wrote and talked throughout the day. Cal made our meals. A few times, he drove me to diners or hole-in-the-wall restaurants he liked. In those places, we talked only about his books or life. I wasn't his lover then; I was the journalist. But at home, he reached for me whenever he wanted. He would toss aside his book and pull me out of my chair, or climb over me in bed, or push me against the tiles in the shower.

There were gentle moments, too, which surprised me more than his lust. Sometimes, he caught my hand or folded me into his arms, kissed me or ran his fingers through my hair. I started to let myself initiate those moments. When I wanted to feel him, I joined him on the couch and curled against his ribs or straddled his lap. He never pushed me away. He sighed, often, and said my name. He liked to grip my hair while he touched me. He liked me to suck on his fingers when he was inside of me.

The profile spilled out as if it had been percolating for weeks. I wove information about his new novel with a cautious narrative of his life, now and before. *The House of Faith* was the key I had needed—something engaging and true, separate from his nightmarish history with Jamie—to provide a framework for the article.

But the novel's conclusion, in which Abigail unraveled and ended up in a psychiatric ward, bothered me on a personal level. It reminded me of what Cal had said about his faith—that it was like his bones and he would break apart without it—and I resented that bleak prospect, because I wanted him to be free. I had a vision of myself tearing him out of his socially imposed cage. That vision changed altogether if the cage became something I had to tear out of him.

"I can't stand the way you ended this," I finally told him one day. We were seated in our usual spots—Cal on the couch, me in an armchair, because closeness was a major distraction—and he was on his laptop. After three days of my presence, he had begun, I thought, to write. He would type and stare into space. He would whisper things to himself.

"Hm?" He looked up from his MacBook.

"This." I gestured with the manuscript. "Abigail falling apart. I don't like it. I want her to succeed without her family. I know she makes some bad choices when she gets away from them, but I want her to . . . triumph, I guess."

"Oh, you want the happy ending." A smile glimmered on his lips.

"Not if it comes off as sentimental. I just think it would be more satisfying."

"Michael, the whole point of the story is that she breaks faith with who she is. She can't triumph. Her family and her faith are her identity."

"People change, though. Life is about changing. I mean, I believed in Santa and the tooth fairy when I was a kid. Leaving that behind didn't crush me."

He chuckled. "God is a little more impressive than the tooth fairy." He was in one of his good moods, when everything made him smile. I decided to go along with it.

"Should I be jealous?"

"Of God?"

"Yeah. Of your obvious infatuation with him."

"Oh, completely." He grinned and stretched out on the couch. I always let him take the couch because he liked to read and even sketch and write lying down, which would have put me to sleep. "We're devoted to each other. Like I said; he's impressive."

"Tell me more."

"About God? All right. He is . . . wealthy beyond your wildest imaginings. Beautiful, powerful, frightening. Passionate. Creative, intelligent. Good. Incredibly demanding and jealous. He doesn't share. He doesn't change. His promises are forever."

"So, he's Christian Grey?"

Cal laughed and shook his head. "If that helps you think about him, sure. But unlike that guy, God is real, and actually worthy of respect and admiration. He's also earnestly obsessed with us, for reasons unclear to me." He tapped a finger against his lips. "Your Christian Grey comparison has some merit, I guess."

I tried, for a moment, to reorient my vision of God from bearded, fatherly guy in the clouds to rich, attractive, domineering CEO. CEO of the universe? Businessmen had never impressed me, though, as most of them seemed greedy and nearly psychopathic.

Cal impressed me. Cal was also most of the things he had described: Beautiful, powerful, passionate, creative, intelligent, good, occasionally frightening. I gazed at him, my head tilted.

"I've never thought about God that way," I said.

He smiled and closed his eyes. "I've never thought about him any other way."

50

CALEB

MICHAEL SPENT A WEEK WITH me, at the expense of his game broadcasts and time with his dog. He also had a series of nightmares from which he woke panting and sweating. When I cornered him about the dreams, he confessed that they involved finding me dead or nearly dead, blood everywhere, my thigh slashed open. He broke down, describing it, and I couldn't bear it. I couldn't bear the fearful way he watched as I left a room, or how he trailed me into every shower or flinched when I used knives to prepare our food.

I couldn't bear to see him in pain.

So, I offered to stay at his place while he worked and took care of his dog. He lunged at the suggestion like a man drowning. I packed a small bag and confined myself to his apartment, which made me feel vaguely claustrophobic, and Furio kept me company while Michael ran twelve-hour game streams and finished the profile.

He was palpably happier, having me close. He would have come unglued, I imagined, if I had insisted we spend time apart.

But I didn't want time apart, either, because Michael was changing me for the better. After a few days in his company, I had stopped trying to suppress my pleasure. He never let me get away without coming. He seemed to know that was the most dangerous time, when I wanted to bleed the desire from my body, and he began to find ways to make me come with him, even before him.

I started to seek out my pleasure, too. My guilt and self-loathing always faded with release, so I drove myself toward climax and then enjoyed Michael's body at my leisure, teasing him, making him wait.

Those days reminded me of my time at the apartment with Jamie: Stolen, blissful, outside of morality. I had strayed into a dream.

We spent four and a half days at Michael's place, which was all I could stand. I felt safer and freer and even less human in the mountains, a part of the thin air and forests. Before we headed back to Red Feather, Michael called his ex-girlfriend and offered to drop off Furio. She gave him a hard time about it, from what I could tell, and then insisted on coming to pick up the dog.

"She's suspicious," Michael told me afterward. "We planned to alternate weeks with Furio and I haven't been around. I think she kind of knows there's . . . something."

"Something." I grinned faintly.

"Someone. Whatever." He looked away. "Anyway, I told her I've just been busy with the profile. Uh, she'll be here in twenty minutes, give or take."

I lowered my book. I mostly read at Michael's; I found it difficult to write there, for no clear reason. "Should I hide under your bed?"

"Oh, no. I don't care." He sounded like he didn't care, and also like he had given the situation some thought. "I don't care if you don't care."

"I'm fine," I said, and I remained sprawled along his couch, reading, until the bell rang. It would have been a lie to say I didn't care, though I understood what Michael had meant. But I did care—about him—and I wanted his ex to know. I didn't fear her. When she stepped into the kitchen and saw me reading in the family room, she backed up a step.

"Oh," she said.

Michael was waiting by the door with Furio on a leash.

I tossed aside my book and joined them in the kitchen. I stood beside him, close enough that our arms touched.

"Hello, Nicole," I said.

"Hi," she chirped. "I didn't know you were here. I guess you guys are still working on that thing, right? The, uh"—she shifted her large handbag and took the leash from Michael—"thing for the . . ." She gestured. She could not compute my presence, barefoot at her ex-boyfriend's apartment at nine in the morning.

"The profile," I supplied, "for *The New Yorker*."

"Yes. Oh my God. I haven't had enough caffeine yet."

"Well, I think there's still some coffee in the pot." I said it as if I lived there, as if I had the right to offer her a cup of coffee, and I saw the moment when it dawned on her—the possibility, the waxing realization, that Michael had discarded her for *me*.

Her head came up and she met my eyes. I gave her my most charming smile. Then she looked at Michael, who was watching the whole encounter in his own private state of shock.

"I'm okay," she stammered. "Gimme a call, Mike, when, uh—we'll figure out next week." She retreated, unable to meet either of our gazes now.

"Sure thing," he said. "Thanks, Nic."

He closed the door and stared up at me.

"Something the matter?" I said.

"I think she . . ." He shook his head. "She's not an idiot, that's all."

I took his jaw in my hand and lifted his face. "I wanted her to know."

His eyes widened a fraction. "Okay."

"I wanted her to know," I repeated, bringing my mouth close to his. "I wanted her to know you're mine. I wanted her to know I'm fucking you." I searched his expression. "I'm proud of you." His breath hitched against my lips. He put a hand on my hip, another on my stomach. I kissed him and backed him into the counter.

He got hard for me so quickly. He was almost excessively sensitive, and I wondered if I owed a debt to Nicole, who had never given him as much attention as I did. As I got on my knees, he tried to tell me that he was proud of me, too, but ecstasy and his general struggle with communication made it difficult.

Still, I understood him. I understood him and I wouldn't have cared if Nicole had returned and found me sucking him off in the kitchen. She deserved to know that I loved what had only ever been a chore to her.

51

MICHAEL

S*OMETHING CHANGED AT MY APARTMENT*, subtly, for the better. Not so long ago, Cal hadn't seemed to want Nicole to know about us. And I had planned to keep us a secret, for his sake, from everyone. After all, I didn't need people to know that we were together; I only needed him, and I wouldn't jeopardize that.

But Cal, of his own volition, had practically exposed our relationship to Nicole. He was changing during intimacy, too. He was letting himself come, seeking it out, he wasn't rushing through sex, and the haunted expression was fading from his face.

When we got back to Red Feather, he built a fire, laid blankets in front of it, and made love to me. Afterward, though it had been obvious in his touch, he gathered me against his chest and said, "I love you now." He made it sound like an oath. I told him I loved him, too, but I don't know if he heard me. He stared into the flames and gripped me tighter. "I love you now," he repeated.

On the occasions we went out together, he seemed more relaxed. He never held my hand or kissed me in public, but he stood close enough that our bodies brushed, he sometimes touched my arm or shoulder, and he let his eyes linger on me the way he did at the house—long and slow, with obvious affection.

One day, at the grocery store, he pressed an avocado into my palm and closed his fingers around mine.

"This one's perfect," he said. "See?"

I smiled and shrugged, pressuring the leathery skin. "Kind of."

"Not too firm, not too soft." His hands moved up to my wrists. "Perfect."

I must have flushed, because he chuckled and studied my face.

"Nobody cares," he remarked on the way home. He glanced at the rearview mirror as if he expected a tail.

"About what?"

"You, me." He sounded far away.

He meant, I realized, something related to his display at the grocery store. I nodded and allowed him to think a while longer. Then I said, "Yeah, it's twenty-sixteen. We've come a pretty long way. It's a good thing."

He didn't agree or disagree.

It was the middle of November and I had completed, revised, and polished the profile. I finally showed it to him. He sat on the couch with my laptop while I chewed on a nail and waited. His dark eyes scanned the screen, he grew still as a stalking cat, and his expression betrayed nothing. A nervous laugh shot out of me.

"We should trade laptops," I said. "I could check out what you're writing."

He glanced at me absently. "Oh, I don't think so, Michael."

"Kidding." I rubbed my palms on my jeans.

"It would be awkward," he murmured.

"Why?"

He continued to read. "It's about you."

"What?"

"I said, it's about you."

"No, I heard. I . . ." I looked at his laptop, its thin silver profile resting innocently on the couch. "I'm surprised, that's all." And I was suddenly, rabidly curious. I wondered what Cal could have to say about me at any length.

"Are you?" He closed my laptop halfway and leveled me with his stare. "I think about you constantly. I wake up thinking about you. I fall asleep thinking about you. I'm always wondering what's on your mind. I wish I could constantly hear your impressions. I think about what sort of gifts you would like, or places we could travel together. Even after we've been in bed . . . I'm immediately fantasizing about other things I want to do to you. Every song I hear seems to be about you. My hand doesn't want to draw anything else. If I pick up an instrument, it's you I'm playing for. When I'm working out, I'm thinking about the way you look at my body, how much I like it. I think about you more than I think about God now. So what else would I write about?"

His confession hit me with physical force. I sank back in the armchair. For weeks, I had thought that my fascination with Cal was one-sided, or maybe it is always impossible to believe that someone else's obsession could match our own. But Cal had essentially described himself through my eyes. *I think about you constantly.*

"Do you use my name?" I blurted out.

He laughed, openly amused by my question. "Always, in first drafts. Whose name do you think I used instead of Abigail? I go back and change it, when I'm done."

I thought about Cal writing *The House of Faith* using his own name instead of Abigail's. "Your family would come around," I said. "If they knew. If you told them."

"You think so?"

"I know they would."

His eyes closed for a while and his smile faded. "You make me believe that, but if you weren't here, I think I wouldn't be able to believe it."

"Well, I'm not going anywhere."

He stirred, as if he were going to get up, and then he went back to reading.

About ten minutes later, he said, "This is very good, Michael."

I exhaled deeply. "Yeah? You like it?"

"I do. I'm impressed. I shouldn't be—I know you're a great writer—but this is very different from your blog. More serious. It's deft and insightful."

The goofiest grin expanded on my face. "Yeah?"

"Yes." He smiled and passed my laptop. "It will be the best of its kind, easily."

"Only because you gave me your book."

"No," he said seriously. "You made it work, given what you could say and what you couldn't. And you kept it objective."

"That wasn't easy." The relief was obvious in my voice. His opinion mattered to me more than anyone else's. "How are the facts?"

He clarified some details and I took notes and implemented them. Then he read it again and said, "You're good to go."

The profile had been our premise for meeting for so long that I felt something cave under me. Relief and happiness gave way to doubt. "Great. I'll . . ." I stared at the document. "I'll send it off, I guess."

He was watching me, reading my face.

"You could stream here, you know."

I blinked a few times. "You want that?"

"Yeah, if the net is good enough. We could get you set up in the guest room, or in my office. I mostly write out here anyway."

My Twitch channel was bleeding subscribers, and, each day I spent in Red Feather, I was losing hundreds of dollars in donations. It made sense for me to return to streaming now that I had finished the profile.

"I think I could make it work with your upload speeds," I said tentatively.

"Good. Anyway, if you can't, I'll stay with you while you stream." He shrugged and went back to writing—writing about me.

I didn't trust my voice just then, so I nodded hurriedly and e-mailed the profile to Eliza Harel at *The New Yorker*.

52

CALEB

Beth's call came the same day that Michael sent in the profile. I knew I should have e-mailed the document to her first, but I had wanted to delay that conversation. As it turned out, I only succeeded in delaying it a few hours.

"My agent," I said to Michael after checking my phone.

He shrank, half-jokingly. "Am I in trouble?"

"You? Never." I tousled his hair on my way past. "I may be, though." I went into the office, but I left the door ajar. Over two weeks had passed since Michael's discovery of my injuries and he still monitored my inner thighs at every opportunity, tracing the healing wounds with his eyes, fingers, and lips.

I wanted those lips on my legs now. I closed my eyes and thought about that as I took Beth's call. "Hi, Beth. That was fast."

"Well." She laughed brusquely. I already knew how she felt: Furious, hurt, and simultaneously afraid to upset me, because I finally had a new book that she imagined she might sell. "I'm speechless, Cal."

"Oh, I doubt that."

"Really. *The New Yorker* was blown away. Is it true?"

"Yes. I read it and approved it. I told the journalist to send it in whenever. I was going to send it to you, of course."

"The profile, or the book?" She laughed again, nerves fraying in her voice.

"The profile, Beth."

"When do I get to see *The House of Faith*? Is it really finished?"

"It is. You know I'm not publishing anymore."

"You have to let me see it, Cal. Do I need to beg?"

I had thought about this conversation, so my answers were ready. "You can read it, but I don't want Mark to see it." Mark was my editor at Doubleday.

"Perfect," she said. "No problem."

"I mean it."

"So do I. I'm excited. I'll be looking for it."

"I'll send it tonight."

"Great."

"I'm sorry," I added. "I was going to send the profile."

"Absolutely no problem." She was on cloud nine now and nothing could pull her down. We said goodbye and Michael appeared in the doorway.

"Everything okay?" he said.

I nodded and smiled lazily at him. A solid seventy percent of my mind was still devoted to his mouth on me. Sometimes, I felt that I had gone so long without intimacy that Michael's arrival in my life had broken a dam. I was oversexed, definitely.

"She wants to read the book." I beckoned, leaning back in the chair and spreading my legs slightly. "Of course."

He slipped into the room and glanced at my crotch. He had a hilarious nervous habit of doing so. "I hope that won't make problems for you."

"No," I mumbled, closing my eyes. I could barely be bothered continuing to talk about books. "I was thinking about your mouth."

Soon enough, he was on his knees, his tongue on my erection. He was getting better at that—getting more comfortable with it. As he sucked, his hand roamed up beneath my shirt, brushing my nipples. I gripped the arms of the chair, my legs shaking.

"Ah . . . good," I whispered. "Michael, it feels so good." I had learned how to compartmentalize my shame, how to set it aside so that I could fully enjoy our time together, and he had learned how to make me wait, how to make me beg.

5 3

MICHAEL

Eliza Harel called me about an hour after Cal's agent called him. We were in bed, where we had moved from the office. And, fortunately, we were finished. In the realm of Very Important Things, sex with Cal rated above a call from *The New Yorker*.

"Your turn," he said presciently when my phone rang. We were lying side by side, aimlessly entwining our fingers and collecting our wits. The room smelled of sex, sweat, and cologne—and there were traces of firewood and oil paint in the air. To me, that combined scent was all Cal, and I loved it.

I snagged my phone and read the screen. "Yup. Wish me luck."

"Luck." He grazed his knuckles along my cheek. He would have kept doing so, I thought, if I hadn't sat up and scooted to the edge of the bed. I wasn't remotely urbane enough to lie in bed caressing my lover while chatting with a major magazine editor.

He chuckled and I glanced over my shoulder. The sunlight hit his eyes and I could see their mahogany hue, which so often appeared black. A healthy, honeyed tone was returning to his skin. He had looked like death when I had first met him. Without love, or sexual satisfaction at the very least, and with only horrific memories for company, he had been—I realized now—dying from the inside out. Despair is as deadly as cancer. It eats at the spirit, which generates our will to live.

But he loved me now. I spontaneously and clearly understood what that declaration had meant. Where God and art had failed him, I had become his *raison d'être*. That great responsibility didn't frighten me. I could actually save him—*was* saving him. It was happening right before my eyes: Life, offering me one rare and perfect miracle.

"Mr. Beck?" Eliza Harel said, maybe not for the first time. I smiled at Cal and turned back toward the window.

Never before, to Eliza Harel, had I been *Mr. Beck*.

So this was what professional success felt like.

"Hi, good afternoon," I said.

"There you are. Well. I don't know where to start. We are *so* thrilled. I just got off the phone with Mr. Bright's agent. They're both on board with the profile. I never"—she stopped short of saying something, then started again—"I knew you were the right choice for this piece. It's . . . incredible. Everyone here is so excited. We're making this the focus for the whole issue." Her gushing paused.

"Th-thank you," I stammered. "I—"

"We're thinking about a few photos—the author, his residence. The fact that he has a new book, and he gave it to you"—another dramatic pause—"and you're letting us break this news. We are *beyond* thrilled. Now, we know you have a blog . . ."

Several seconds passed before I processed her meaning.

"Oh. I won't be writing about it there. It's all yours."

"Wonderful. Excellent. We *will* be in touch, Mr. Beck. You can expect to hear from me next month, okay? We have a lot of ideas for twenty-seventeen."

I thanked her and said goodbye. My ears were ringing. Eliza Harel was a fast talker with a brassy voice, which got faster and brassier when she was *beyond* thrilled.

"Impressive pipes on that lady," Cal said. He was still lying in bed, an arm behind his head and his eyes closed.

I laughed. "Yeah, no kidding."

"She sounded happy."

"For sure." I scooted closer to him, a bright smile stuck to my mouth. "I think you, uh, single-handedly launched my journalism career."

"It wasn't all me. You wrote the profile."

I gazed at his unperturbed features. "The book made the profile."

"Let's call it fifty-fifty," he said.

One of the things I loved about Cal: He was a realist.

"Sixty-forty." I nestled against his flank. He sighed contentedly and found my hand, folding our fingers against his chest. "They are . . . crazy excited."

"I'm sure they think I'll go on to publish it."

"I wish you could."

His fingers tensed. "It's fine."

It wasn't *fine* to me, though. One day, I wanted Cal's life to be more than us—to contain everything he deserved: Faith, family, love, and professional success. It was unfair for my career to be going places because of a brilliant book that he couldn't publish, because of a bigoted, psychotic shrew of a woman. Cal thought he had killed Jamie, but Coral had killed Jamie. She had as good as tied the noose.

I took a few deep breaths for composure.

No, that wasn't right, either. Jamie had killed himself. Cal's ex-wife wasn't innocent, though. She was a monster from a fairytale, unbelievable in her horror.

"You can't . . . let her do this." The words came out weak, but at least I spoke them. "Have you ever thought about using a pen name?"

He moved off the bed, dressing briskly. "No. That thought never crossed my mind. Not once in the last four years."

I winced. He hadn't slung cynicism at me in a long time and it hurt more than it had before. "Sorry. I just—"

"You know what's at stake for me. You think I would take chances with that?"

"No. You're right."

"And I don't want to start over, Michael. I'm Caleb Bright. I have some pride."

"I get that."

"Do you? I don't want to publish. Not under my name or any name. I'm done with all that. There are consequences to things. You wouldn't understand."

"You're right, I don't understand." I began to dress, too, my face hot with frustration and embarrassment. I was his lover now. He couldn't keep treating me like the journalist, like the little nobody, second to him. "I will never understand. All that shit—it only makes sense to you. You have options. You could take her to court."

He gave me a dark, frightening stare, and then he headed downstairs.

I went after him almost immediately.

He was smoking on the deck, looking knotted up and aloof, which I hadn't seen in weeks. I waited a while before going out. The air was bitterly cold, the lake frozen and snowed over, and neither of us was wearing a jacket. I laid my forehead gently on his shoulder. He turned and embraced me fiercely with one arm.

"I'm sorry," he said.

I hugged him around the middle, my face hidden against his neck. "Don't be."

"No, I am. I want to be that for you—the bestselling author. Whatever you want. I get so angry, Michael, I think about killing her. It's like acid, getting that angry. I must be bleached inside. I feel that way."

I had never seen Cal cry and I didn't want to, and he sounded close.

"I don't need you to be a bestselling author," I said. "You already are. I just want you to do what you love and have success."

"I need my family more." Grief thinned his voice. "It's like, if they don't know, God doesn't know. And I want to go to Heaven." He sounded like a little boy, lost and scared, and he told me how terrified he was of being forgotten as an author, and he told me how he used to cut himself out of sheer frustration, for having ruined his own life.

"Okay," I said, holding him tight and stroking his hair and back. "Okay."

54

CALEB

A PHOTOGRAPHER CAME TO MY house at the end of November and shot black and whites for the profile. Michael was with me. I introduced him as "Michael Beck, the journalist," and the photographer shook his hand enthusiastically.

The man took dozens of photos. Afterward, he brought them up on his laptop and we selected our favorites. I looked better than I had in a long time, less haggard, more focused, confident, and calm.

"I like that one." Michael pointed to an image of me on the deck. It was a back shot, sky and mountains framing my figure, a cigarette listing from my hand.

"That one," I said indifferently, and the photographer moved it to a folder.

We selected another, a portrait photo, in which I stared unsmilingly at the viewer, my hands folded under my chin and my hair loose against my face. Looking at that, I understood how I had sometimes intimidated Michael, early on. Even still, though we barely argued anymore, he occasionally withdrew from my gaze.

"I want the rest of them," he whispered to me as the photographer was packing up. "Do you think that's allowed?"

I shrugged and asked the man, who had already prepared a flash drive for me.

"They're all yours," he said, "as long as they're for personal use."

When the photographer left, I gave the flash drive to Michael, who hugged me as if I had given him the keys to a Maserati.

The profile ran in December, as planned. It hit the literary world like a pebble in still water, small in itself, but effecting ever-widening circles. Beth relayed calls and interview requests from a stream of papers and magazines, including *The New York Times,* the *LA Times,* and *The Atlantic.* I turned them down. I had nothing more to say than what I had told Michael, and I wanted his piece to remain one of a kind.

Beth read *The House of Faith* and undertook a personal campaign to get me to publish it. She made herself ridiculous in the process, falling on words like *genius* and *groundbreaking,* and she got me angry enough to level a threat. We had exchanged at least a dozen e-mails and half as many phone calls on the topic and I finally said, "I need an agent who respects my wishes."

And that was that. She stopped pressing and pushing and pestering, and it was a huge relief. As for Michael, we had only argued about the book's future once, which had been one too many times for both of us.

In the absence of facts, the media outlets ran specious headlines: **Caleb Bright Teases New Novel**; **Caleb Bright Breaks Four-Year Silence**; *The House of Faith* **Rumored Release in 2017**. The headlines were click-bait; the articles themselves rehashed material from Michael's profile and conjectured desperately.

I paid those articles no mind, though they unsettled me, the way they were disseminating lies. Maybe I should have gone after them. Maybe I shouldn't have given Michael the book. Maybe I should never have opened the door to Michael.

The problem with second-guessing yourself is that you usually do it too late.

55

MICHAEL

Cal's landline rang late one evening. It almost never rang—I had forgotten it existed—so the noise startled me, and it disturbed me, I don't know why. It was the middle of December and I was streaming from his basement, where he had converted the guest bedroom into a second office for me. He was upstairs, probably reading or writing.

I had finally learned to trust him not to gouge open his leg the moment he got out of my sight. We were doing well—so well that it felt surreal.

The phone rang and rang, and people watching my stream told me to answer it.

"Nah," I said, glancing at the chat. "It's probably a sales call."

Why isn't your girlfriend answering it? a viewer typed.

I ignored the question and continued to play DayZ.

When I had started streaming from Cal's basement, viewers had instantly noticed the change of location. Viewers always acted strangely entitled to information about my life, as if we were in anything but a business relationship. I had explained that my "living situation was in flux" and that I would be streaming from two different locations, and the consensus had been that I was dating someone new. They assumed it was a girl.

I shifted off my headset and listened. Purposeful footfalls crossed the floor overhead and a door closed. Then silence.

"Actually, I'm gonna make sure I didn't miss an important call," I said. "And it's pretty late, dudes, so I'm ending the stream here for tonight." I rattled off my concluding spiel and played my outro. An ominous sensation, like a cold sweat, broke over me as I bounded up the basement steps.

Cal and I may have been doing well, but I still woke sometimes from a nightmare that I couldn't get to him, that he was bleeding, or that he was gone. Seeing him handle knives still bothered me. Light under the bathroom door still made my heart race.

I found Cal in his office, cell to ear. He was sheet white and shaking.

"What's going on?" I said.

His eyes, when they panned to me, were wide with panic.

He lowered his phone and stared at the screen, and then he ended whatever call he was trying to place. I wanted to tell him that he was scaring me, but I could see that he was scared, too, and I didn't want to add to that.

"Hey, tell me what happened." I made my voice calm and I went to him, resting my hands on his shoulders.

"Not sure," he said, the words barely audible. He reached across the desk and hit a button on the answering machine. A male voice, tinged with a southern accent and slurring, said, "Not gonna answer? I know what you did to my brother, you faggot. If I ever run into you, I'll kill you." The message ended with a click.

56

CALEB

ONLY MY SISTER ANSWERED, IN the end. Coral and my parents had blocked my number and their landlines went to answering machines. But Rachel picked up.

"Cal?" she said. Her voice was already breaking.

"Yeah. Hey." I clutched my phone with both hands. Michael lingered in the doorway. I swiveled toward the desk for a little privacy. "Thanks for answering."

"Well . . . yeah."

I hunched forward, a profound feeling of nausea rising up my throat. "Mom and Dad aren't answering. I got a call from . . . well, you remember Jamie Foust." I wiped a slick of perspiration off my brow. "His brother."

"Cal, I know," she said. "I know."

My bones seemed pinned together with tacks. One wrong move and I was going to collapse. "Did Coral . . . do something?"

"She told us. About Jamie. Me, um, his parents. Mom and Dad." A door closed. Rachel spoke in a low voice. I could envision her trying to hide our conversation from her husband. She wasn't supposed to talk to me. "How could you do that? She showed us . . ." Her voice shuddered and halted.

I remembered the photos that Coral's private investigator had taken, of Jamie and I kissing, having sex, and doing other things nobody should ever have seen. Instead of heating, my skin turned cadaver cold.

"I don't know." I blinked rapidly. "Rachel, I don't know. It just . . . happened."

"We could have helped you. Why didn't you tell us?"

"I don't know." I covered my face.

"We would have gotten you help."

"I know."

"That boy who showed up at your house?" Her voice became suddenly unyielding. "The one who came inside when I was there?"

I couldn't deny it. She knew what I had done to Jamie and she knew I was still doing it with Michael, who bore such a strange and strong resemblance to Jamie.

After a long silence, she said, "I have to go."

"Please, don't. Can we talk tomorrow?"

I heard a quick, jagged inhale, the kind that comes before a sob. I knew she was going to hang up and that I would never talk to her again—not unless I got the *help* she had mentioned. I also knew that sort of help would not work for me.

What was inside of me could not be destroyed. I needed Michael like I had needed Jamie. And when I had been without, at Harvard when I was dating Coral long-distance, I used to go to the campus library and pour over the illustrated volumes on Roman and Grecian sculpture. That had been as close as I let myself get—the marble nudes of men with angelic faces and strong, lean bodies, their genitals on shameless display. My mouth used to water and my hands would sweat.

"I'm your brother," I said desperately. "I love you."

She hung up. She didn't have the courage to say goodbye.

And really, I couldn't blame her.

57

MICHAEL

CAL'S FAMILY CUT HIM LOOSE as ruthlessly and completely as he had told me they would. I couldn't believe it until I saw it. And even then, it was difficult to believe. He made dozens of frantic calls and sent as many e-mails, and radio silence returned. The only communication he received was the drunken death threat from Jamie Foust's oldest brother, who must have sobered up and realized that his message constituted a criminal offense, because even the Foust family uniformly blocked Cal's efforts at contact.

"Let's stop trying," I said, as if we were doing anything together. In reality, I was wringing my hands and hovering while he hurled himself against his family's incalculable cruelty. "Things will settle. They *will* come around."

He agreed mindlessly, and then he tried to call them again, several times apiece.

It was like the first day after I had discovered his self-harming. I felt I couldn't let him out of my sight, for fear he would try to hurt himself. But, rather than crushed, Cal was energized by the certainty that he could fix things with his family.

The same night he got the message from Jamie's brother, he poured us each a drink and paced in front of the couch. He was wild-eyed, gesturing manically, and oblivious to me except insofar as I presented a sounding board.

He talked about Coral—how she must have read the misleading headlines regarding his novel, how she must have assumed he was publishing—and hatched and trashed one plan after another. He would threaten her legally. He would talk her down. Somehow, he would make her admit to falsifying the claims and photos.

"I'm sorry," I said. "I'm so sorry, Cal."

I don't know who felt worse, Cal or myself. He wouldn't accept my apology, though. "She got the wrong idea," was all he would say, and, "If I can make her see that I'm not publishing, she'll take it back."

As if any of it could be taken back.

"You *could* publish now," I ventured. I was hoping, recklessly, that he might be relieved. His secret was out, and it may have cost him his family, but it also freed him to pursue his career or demand shared custody of his son. It freed him to be with me, in front of everyone. "You're free," I said earnestly.

I put down my drink and reached for him.

He looked right through me.

5 8

MICHAEL

CAL BARELY SLEPT FOR TWO nights in a row. He lay in bed, his heart pulsing audibly and his back a braid of muscle, and then he got up at four and benched weights until sweat soaked his skin. I followed him. I don't know if he noticed me.

In the shower, he let me hold him and touch him, but his sex drive, understandably, was absent. I took over meal-making duty. He smoked more than he ate and went for long walks in the deep snow, with me stumbling after him.

And then he bought a plane ticket to visit his family.

His mood, which had wavered up and down for three days, lifted with his new plan to show up at his parents' house.

"Are you sure that's a good idea?" I said.

"I don't have any better idea." He smiled gently at me. "And this way, they have to see me. I'll rent a car and drive down to Coral's, too."

"Getting a lawyer might be a better idea."

He gestured negligently. "I don't want any of that. Things are already too ugly."

I pictured Cal ringing his parents' doorbell and standing in the cold, waiting and waiting. "What if they call the cops?"

"Don't be ridiculous."

"I'm serious. The way they've . . ." I trailed off, unwilling to remind him of his family's stonewall.

"They aren't monsters. They're uncompromising in their beliefs."

I could have pointed out that their uncompromising beliefs made them behave like monsters, but this was the best conversation I'd had with Cal in three days and I didn't want to upset him. He was calm and clear-eyed. He was neither irrationally excited nor catatonically depressed, and he seemed to be seeing me again, gazing at me like I was his lover and not just another meaningless object in his house.

"I want to go with you," I said, already knowing I couldn't.

His smile turned faintly sad. "I wish."

"I could hide. Stay at a hotel."

"It's best I go alone. I might get one chance, and if they find out you're with me . . ." He grimaced, apologetic.

I was part of the problem for Cal. If, by some miracle, he did manage to smooth things over with his family, I would have to go away or become even more of a secret. I would be less than a shadow in his life. Or maybe he intended to get rid of me; maybe he had already made up his mind.

"What is it?" he said.

I glared at my feet. "Do you want me gone? I can go away, if you want." The strength in my voice was bravado. "This shit is my fault. The profile."

"Could you go?" For the first time in days, he reached for me. I melted into his touch. He stroked my hair and kissed my forehead, and he brought my head under his chin. I remember thinking: He's the strong one, even now. "No, you can't go away," he said softly. "I thought about asking you. I can't. So don't lie to me. You can't, either."

He rubbed my back and thighs, pressing me closer with each pass of his hands. "When you met me . . ." His fingers pushed under my shirt. I clung to his shoulders while he caressed my sides, my chest and stomach. I went far back in my thoughts—back to my fall on his walkway, his anger and intensity. Maybe he was back there, too. "Well, it's not your fault," he whispered finally. "I wanted to do it. I would do it again."

59

MICHAEL

CAL LEFT ON A MONDAY morning. He headed to the airport in Denver, having declined my offer to take him, and I drove back to my apartment. It was the first time we had been apart in over a month, and we had agreed not to text, call, or e-mail during his trip, on the off chance his family intercepted a communication.

So I wouldn't know how things were going or if he needed me, and I couldn't know if he used the time alone to hurt himself.

He seemed to be in good spirits when he left, though. He had an air of confidence about him, which proceeded, I assumed, from the hope of repairing his relationships. I liked seeing him that way—so sure of himself.

But I didn't like the fact that he had felt the need to get a haircut before his trip. When he had emerged from the barbershop, trying to look happy and running his hands through his close-cropped hair, I had hated his family completely.

He was supposed to return on Friday. That afternoon, I checked my phone incessantly. His flight had arrived on time and I had expected a text or call from the airport, but nothing came. I called his cell and landline—no answer. After several hours, I drove up to his house. The windows were dark. Pristine snow covered the drive.

When I tried the front door and found it unlocked, I guess I knew, because I ran inside and started to shout for him. I checked every bathroom, every closet. The note was on his office desk. He had printed my name on the envelope.

I read it then, I think. It's difficult to remember. I dialed 911. They found him in a deer blind two miles from the house. An ambulance took me to the ER and I checked myself in to the psychiatric ward. He had shot himself in the head with a handgun I hadn't known he owned. He had never taken the flight east. He had driven away, turned back, and gone to the deer blind so that I would not find him. And that was the hardest part: Knowing that he was alone in the end, outside in the cold, afraid, alone, that he had to be uncomfortable, sitting in a frozen deer blind, his beautiful hair gone.

60

CALEB

December 2016

Dearest Michael,

Listen to me. Don't be afraid. Don't panic; for me, don't panic. I'm holding you. Remember that feeling. I'm moving over you forever.

This is the only thing I can do and I don't expect you to forgive me, but I am sorry. I have two loves fighting inside of me and I can't live without you and I can't live without God. So I can't live. When you aren't so angry and sad, I know you will understand.

I need your strength now. I'm afraid of the pain. I'm thinking about you in the annex, taking my hand and putting it on your body for the first time. I'm thinking about the morning sun in your hair. It is you I will be thinking about in the end—you, Michael, until I can't think—my angel for the last phase.

Cal

Printed in Great Britain
by Amazon